I0453067

The Clocks of London

Waters of London, Volume 1

Pamela Lyn and Lyn Brittan

Published by Gryy Brown Press, 2014.

The Clocks of London
Copyright 2014 © Pamela Lyn/Lyn Brittan
Editing by Victoria Anderson Baksa
www.lynbrittan.com

Also by Pamela Lyn

Cape Elizabeth Series
The Prince
The Traitor
The Chosen
The Wolves of Cape Elizabeth: The
Complete Series
Alecto

Lightning Saga
Rafe's Reward
Qiang's Quest
Juan's Journey
Scott's Solace
Lightning Saga Bundle

Waters of London
The Clocks of London

Watch for more at www.pamelalyn.com.

Also by Lyn Brittan

Cape Elizabeth Series
The Prince
The Traitor
The Chosen
Alecto

Lightning Saga
Rafe's Reward
Qiang's Quest
Juan's Journey
Scott's Solace

Outer Settlement Agency
Solia's Moon
Anja's Star
Quinn's Quasar
Lana's Comet
Outer Settlement Agency Omnibus
Vin's Rules
Anja's Star

The Djinn Series
The Genie's Witch
A Genie's Love
The Cowboy Genie's Wife

Waters of London
The Clocks of London
The Doctor of London

Standalone
Moonlit Embrace

Watch for more at www.lynbrittan.com.

To Mom - Yes, I make people kiss.

THE CLOCKS OF LONDON

The Waters of London
By
Lyn Brittan writing as Pamela Lyn
Website | Mailing List

Chapter I

London, 1888

Moira Gear clasped her hands to keep them from shaking on the morning submarine out of Brighton to London. Her gaze shifted from one side of the vessel to the other and she leaned against threadbare seats. The last time she'd traveled in a vessel this size, they'd had pressed linen-covered tables, silver utensils and plates of steaming hot food.

Not this time.

She pressed against a porthole, desperate for something cool on her cheek. Could the perspiration she wiped from her brow be a result of the humidity regulator gone awry?

No, probably not.

Just fear.

Around her, other passengers read newspapers and puffed on foul-smelling pipes. Cheap tobacco? She hadn't thought it existed. The rare crop took ages to reach London from the above-water countries. Her father's oyster pipe carried the aroma of heaven and chestnuts. The filth these men expelled stank of burst sewage pipes.

Moira took a kerchief from her reticule and wiped a smidgen of grime from the window. *Ugh.* She'd taken plenty of real submarines in her life. This one wasn't fit to transport trash to the surface. What kind of passenger vessel had portholes instead of proper windows?

Still, there was nothing to be done for it. In this new life of hers, a cheap, chugging, creaking and limping sub made the most financial sense. Being born to money and surviving without it were ever so different.

Home.

She dabbed the corners of her eyes at the memory of it. Her family lived off their name and lines of credit. When he had no servant available to carry currency, Father waved his hand, dropped his calling card and had the bill sent straight to the Royal Bank or his secretary. She no longer had such options of the purse. When she'd left this morning, she did so with only the gold, silver and fruit seeds she'd found around the house...

And her father's library. And her brother's office.

She toed her red paisley satchel on the floor. It wasn't theft. The jewels, the fig seeds, all of it comprised part of her inheritance. Family property really. She had every right to it.

Most of it.

Some of it.

Small bit.

"Tea and paper, Miss?" A besmocked porter wheeled his squeaking cart over.

Moira raised her hand, but shook her head and sent the boy away. Best to save her money and get used to doing without. Every single half pence mattered now.

Her eyes flittered over the daily held by the man in front of her. She couldn't make out the words of the newspaper from this angle, but she didn't need to. No doubt, it would have a story of another missing child from London.

The small text likely lay buried deep between articles concerning the latest fashions from the gilded sea walls of Paris and notices of who met whom at this botany lecture or wore what at a golden ball.

No one ever spoke about them, save her. She read the daily every day and noticed issues. Strange issues. Missing children sort of issues.

These children came from full households on the lower levels of London, the side avenues where city transport didn't go and where no one had access to the water's surface. The authorities wouldn't care about missing lower-class boys. The papers hadn't even bothered to add their names most times. Parents of such children didn't have the means to hire proper investigators, either. That's where she came in.

She'd investigate, solve the problem, and become the heroine she intended to be whilst proving to her brother that she'd make a dynamic partner in his investigative firm. Not that he alone needed convincing. It was well and fine for Michael to abandon tradition and work on saving the streets, but the moment she'd asked to participate in what he was building, three events happened in rapid and terrible succession. Her mother fainted dead away, her father slammed his fist into the wall hard enough to send nearby fish scattering, and her brother laughed. The latter stung the most.

"You've saved me from being the black sheep," he'd said and walked out the door.

He hadn't been wrong on that account.

"Lovely day, in'int, Missus?"

Moira nodded to the girl next to her on the tattered bench. Her clothes appeared frayed but clean. Her reticule, a pale green, may have once been the deeper tone of the girl's dress several washings ago. "It is indeed. Moira Gear, private investigator."

The young woman's lips parted into a small O, and her eyes widened to tea saucers. "Matilda, but everyone calls me Maggie. A lady copper? I ain't never heard of such. Do you carry a loaded barker and everything? You kill anyone dead wi'it? How long you been doing that?"

I started today didn't sound entirely convincing. "It runs in the family."

"Strange family. Beggin' your pardon, ma'am." Maggie leaned forward and dropped her voice several registers. "Is that what it's about? I know your type didn't belong on this submarine. Is there a case? A murderer here, among us?"

"No, that's not quite what I said. I've –"

"An actual murderer?"

"No..." But whatever theater played in Maggie's mind gave a smashing performance. Despite her rather forceful protestations, the girl's voice rose to shrill and desperate levels. Surrounding passengers dropped any pretense of not listening and leaned forward with whispers and pointed fingers.

"Maggie, there's no fuss. There aren't any murderers on this submarine. I'm here to investigate missing children."

"Wh...what? Someone's kidnapping little lords and ladies?" She may as well have screamed in the cabin. Murmurings of conversation ceased and newspapers crinkled as they were folded into laps.

"Actually, no. No one would let that happen. It's the small children. Tunnel children – the ones without parents or a home. The ones who've probably never left the water. Poor things, imagine, only knowing artificial light and never going above to land?"

"Do you mean to say, Miss, that you're here on account of chavvies? Who cares about the little mouchers?"

And that put voice to her challenge. No one did. Not even a country bumpkin like Maggie could spare a thought. Conversation resumed throughout the cabin and people went on with their business, happy to ignore the children of the tunnels.

"You know, they say that in London, they have concourses and tunnels so deep that you can't see outside for nothing."

"I'm sure they have lighting of some sort, Maggie."

"But them's is deep."

"Impossible. Anything below three thousand meters would be unstable. Pressure would crush the tunnels and everyone inside. The seabed doesn't go that low here, even if they could build them in the first place. I assure you, we're as safe in the tunnels of

London as we are anywhere else. They're built upon the islands of old Britannia."

"Oh, I hope so, Missus. First time too? I heard their main station can hold a thousand subs and shuttles at once."

"That's a slight exaggeration."

"It ain't. They say that the port it's attached to goes up and up above water and that you can dock a hundred boats to it on the surface. Mul-ti-lev-el," she said, enunciating each syllable with a nod.

"According to records, that simply isn't the case. It is large, but—"

"And they say..."

Maggie rattled down her list of *I heard* and *they said* until a claxon signaled their imminent arrival. The sound sent the girl into a giggling tizzy. She leaned over to look out the tiny window until her greasy hair caught on Moira's lips.

"Would you care to switch seats?"

"Iffin' you don't mind."

She did. They approached her new home too, but as much as her northern companion annoyed her, she couldn't fault Maggie's excitement. She hadn't visited here since she was fourteen. Five years later through a fingerprint-stained porthole, it looked just as glorious.

Moira turned, but Maggie stood up and grabbed her belongings, stretching her neck and popping over the shoulders of others on raised toes. Perhaps some of what she'd said had been right. Moira had disembarked at Gatwick, a busy but aged hub, those many years ago. She now arrived at Heathrow, a station as grand as they'd said.

While the submarine linked to dock, glass bottoms of boats in the not-too-far distance pulled into an above-water station. Odd to see, but it made perfect sense. Land-born foreigners would have to come into the city that way for proper pressurization.

A child waved furiously and she waved back in answer, grinning so hard her cheeks started to quiver. She couldn't make out any of the child's features beyond bobbing curls, but it didn't matter. London welcomed them all. Even those like the child above, who'd have to wait days to properly enter her grand and glittering halls.

It wasn't until the door opened and she exited the sub that it hit her. That here in the great crush and cacophony of people, she was very much alone. She had no one to point out fine tiling on the floor or to stare at rare London stingrays swimming so close to the overhead glass that their fins brushed against the walls.

Her chest throbbed at the loss, ticking in time with the gigantic clock towering above her.

She missed her family. Even Michael. But she couldn't go home until she'd proven her worth, and she couldn't do that standing around. With one last solidifying breath, she clutched her bags, found a way map and selected one of hundreds of tunnels that formed the connected roads of Water London.

Chapter II

"So, Mr. Clock, will you help me find my son?"

Patrick rose to stand by the pearl-trimmed window. A red and yellow cuttlefish traced his movements as he paced alongside the clear wall. "Please, call me Patrick. And yes, I will. So you think he's fallen in with the wrong crowd. Any ideas, Mr. McCoy, why would he leave this wonderful life behind to sleep in the tunnels?"

"Damned if I know, and what does it matter?"

"It could mean everything." Patrick took a swig of his brandy and shrugged. "Before you get the wheres, you need to gather the whys."

"I hardly see the point." The grey-haired man gathered his neatly chevron-shaped beard in his hands and leaned back into a leather chair.

Yes, leather – the most expensive fabric in the waters. A leather chair behind a mahogany desk. Patrick tried counting the rings in the wood and gave up. If the man could afford such luxury, why hire him? He was good, but there were other options.

"This will require your full discretion."

"I see." And he did. Most of his cases involved wayward wives and contested wills. Not the sort of subject that made the scandal pages of local rags. Those cases brought in decent money, but never enough. Back in his grandmother's day, finding clients hadn't been a problem. Since her death, however, he'd struggled to fill the massive shoes of the Clock name. Something this big could do it. Not that the well heeled talked openly about such things – but word would get whispered around.

Hell. He had the word. He needed the money. Until he met all the conditions of Matron Clock's will, he'd have to quickstep from one case to the next and earn it the hard way.

"So?"

"So? Tell me. Can't be that bad. Or is it? Your face—"

"Are you mocking me, sir?"

"Certainly not my intent, but I have a nasty habit of getting a feel for the waters before I swim. Why did your son leave?"

"Private matters. Some doxy. Beneath him." McCoy filled his glass a third time. Dark liquid splashed over the edges and the bottle rattled against the table. Patrick turned away, giving the man his privacy.

Palsy.

Shame. The man couldn't be more than fifty. Too young to have the shakes.

"Don't act as if you haven't noticed. It's why I've avoided society. You know how they are. They see a drop of blood in the water and attack. That's why that boy needs to stand up. He's twenty-two years old. I need him here, not laid out beneath some cheap ladybird. He's to inherit a company, and more than that, a title. The sop's unworthy of both."

"Yet he is your son."

"If not him, then my brother. I have my pick of reprobates. Will you help me or not?"

"Three hundred pounds."

To his credit, McCoy didn't gasp. He didn't do much of anything other than take another swig. "Robbery, but I'm desperate."

"You're rich enough. I should have asked for more."

The elder man laughed and raised his glass in toast. For the first time during their meeting, he sipped instead of guzzled. The mention of money had a tendency to do that. "Quite, quite. I have faith in you, boy. You can't be much older than my Samuel, but you've managed respectability."

"In my line of work? Coming from a man like you, that's high praise indeed."

"All work is noble. The title I was born into, but the money? Not so much. I put in a lot of hours for every coin I've made. Your job is to ensure it's not gone to waste. I expect a report soon."

Patrick knew a dismissal when he heard one and choked down the last of his sinfully good drink. A stack of currency appeared on the edge of the desk before he put down the emptied glass. To avoid dishonoring McCoy by doing more, he conducted a lazy count, which showed about half of the payment. Unstated, he knew he'd get the rest with the return of the boy.

Patrick bowed, retrieved his derby from the butler in the hallway and stepped out onto the passageways of London.

The McCoys resided in one of the best tunnels in the labyrinth. His line of work had taken him to some of the worst, but instead of vermillion-decked working girls and pullcart wagon-cycles, everyone here walked at a leisurely pace or rode in private litters on the backs of servants. It wasn't too dissimilar from his home, though he preferred his bicycle to anything else.

He hopped onto it and pedaled toward the main hubs of first Gatwick then Heathrow. Most companies kept notices of travelers. It would take an age, but he meant to look into their recent passenger lists for any sign of the McCoy boy.

Privacy meant a lot in this town. Coins went a bit farther. Another reason he required money at the beginning of his investigations – bribery almost always aided him in solving them.

He pinched his nose at the thought of digging though stacks of books. A headache was coming. His traitorous mind did that at the mere thought of words. Just words. Odd enough, not the letters themselves. Hell of a curse, to enjoy the word puzzles in the dailies but ache at the articles surrounding them.

The bike skidded to a stop halfway to the center of the city, near a part of town where private litters disappeared and policemen worked two to a beat.

He'd do better to farm out this part of the investigation to Kennerick. The good doctor needed to pull some more of the weight anyway.

He'd angled the wheels of his cycle to take a shortcut when a series of screams echoed off the brightly painted buildings. Naturally, he ran toward it.

He had to fight his way to the front of the growing horde, past fainting women and shouting men. The cause of the ruckus laid in the center – a boy dead in the street with a line of blood trailing from his nose to the ground.

Officers so new that their badges still glinted raised their hands to push aside the gawkers. This was a largely unsuccessful enterprise, but it gave Patrick time to work.

Male. Young. No more than ten years of age.

Face? Dirty. Nails? Ragged. Hands?

Hands.

Blood pooled in the lad's palms. Not a lot, but enough to recognize defensive wounds. But here? Patrick searched from side to side to get his bearings on this end tunnel. No, it wasn't a main thoroughfare, but it touched one close enough that he wouldn't expect someone to get away with murder. To what end?

The torn clothes and bare feet left it fairly clear that he wasn't dealing with a failed kidnapping for ransom. Could the child have been a thief? Sure. But why kill him? It didn't sit right. A thief this young could be shoved aside or held for arrest. A person didn't attack and strike a killing blow. Someone wanted the boy silenced, but why? That said, the killer might want to stand around to ensure success in the deed.

Still crouching, Patrick turned to survey the crowd. Looks of horror. Looks of interest. Looks of twisted delight. None of these held his attention. He searched each face for one expression – relief.

Not present.

He did, however, encounter one that kept his gaze locked firmly in place.

Clinical.

Analytical.

Angelic.

It belonged to a woman so beautiful that his breath caught in his throat. Could it be *her*?

An upturned nose scrunched as she glanced from the boy to sheets of paper. The woman's pencil moved furiously, like algae eaters scrambling along the outer walls. She was, in fact, the sole woman not fainting, recovering from a faint, or pretending to faint.

He didn't bother to hide his stare. She didn't notice him. She couldn't. The woman's eyes went to two places, the child and her papers. Her interest made no sense. She wore a black and blue traveling dress, lightly bustled and draped – one built for walking and yet prim and absolutely proper. A matching series of genuine feathers dotted hair pulled into a loose coil at her nape. A rich woman in a lower-class tunnel taking notes on a dead boy sent too many wrong signals.

He inched closer, studying features that grew more familiar by the second.

Umber skin, dimpled cheeks and lips pinched as she worked.

Moira Gear.

He pushed on for confirmation. Dear heavens, it was her! Years had changed her from a girl to a stunning beauty of a woman. But what the devil did she do here? He'd seen her often enough while still at university. She was the sister of his old classmate, Michael. The wee, quiet girl had never wandered far from her mother's skirts. He'd wanted permission to call upon her so long ago but always lost the nerve.

So where were her parents now?

Half of him rebelled, not wanting to take his eyes off her. Yet he forced himself to survey the crowd for her family. They weren't here.

He couldn't very well leave her alone. "Ms. Gear?"

Women close to him turned, but she appeared too engaged in her task to attend him. He kept pushing, each time making his way closer. Sirens sounded and police wagon-cycles pounded down the street. The racket stopped as one of the officers jumped down, shaking his siren-ringing arm as he did. The crowd parted for the influx of uniforms, but Patrick stood on the wrong side, now more separated from the woman than ever before.

Police hustled the boy, wrapped in a white sheet, onto the wagon before pedaling away. Patrick ought to stay and investigate as the crowd dispersed, but Miss Gear broke into a run, following the police wagon down the street.

The devil?

This was no delicate, feet-of-glass skip. The woman hitched up her dress and held onto her papers and pencil with one hand while gripping her luggage with the other. Not following was *not* an option. But even with her bundle, she moved faster than frenzied skippers. He raised his hands and called out to stop her.

Bad idea.

Michael's sister turned, then ran as though the devil nipped her feet. He recognized her fear, but not the cause. Him? Or getting caught?

She took a side tunnel, one connecting to Main.

"Stop! Please, Miss Gear, stop!"

Papers fluttered around her as she increased her pace. She didn't look back anymore – she simply ran. If he didn't catch her before she reached that corner, he'd lose her entirely, swallowed by the great populace of London.

Chapter III

She was so mad she could spit! There was only one person to blame for this.

Chased like a thief in the street? Oh, curse her brother.

Moira climbed the stairs of the boarding house, careful not to touch the walls and their suspect stains. In dim lighting, she strained to place her steps, avoiding slick spots and rotten, half-eaten pieces of food. It took a lot of swallowing to keep going.

Swallowing of bile.

Swallowing of pride.

The owners let the room at two pound a night – it and its shared bath and one half window.

She took a solidifying breath and stuck her key in the door. Not much to inventory on the other side.

One bed with brown sheets. Correction, sheet.

One table with an empty glass flipped on its side.

One chamber basin.

So ended the list of her new belongings in her new life.

She opened her suitcase, laid a shawl across the thin sheet and collapsed onto the bed. She'd have to sleep in layers if she meant to stay warm tonight, though she hardly had sleeping on the schedule. Her case, and the unexpected chase, plagued her.

Two things dueled for attention and thoughts of her less-than-heavenly living quarters drifted away. The poor boy dead in the street and that strange man who had studied him intently. He'd had the focused attention of an inspector. She'd seen that sharpened eye on her brother plenty of times. That's where the similarity ended. The dark man was far more handsome, though he looked oddly familiar.

Yet because of her brother, she knew he couldn't have been investigating that boy. The sharp-cheeked man wore better clothes than inspectors. Gentleman's clothes. Not as fine as her father's for sure, but respectable.

And if he wasn't there to investigate the boy, then he was there to investigate her. This had Michael's name written all over it. How had he found her so quickly? Her brother was good – better than she thought. But not better than her. She'd escaped and that had her smiling. Then she leaned over, took in her surroundings and the smile dripped right onto the lumpy mattress.

Yes, her brother...*oh brother!*

She sat straight up, the slow cogs in her mind clicking into place. The man was the student who stayed across the hall from Michael at boarding school! Not any student.

Him.

The one who'd smiled so sweetly behind his hands.

He'd grown.

Substantially.

Gone was the boy with long lashes and skin the color of a boat's hull at night. Today, the man had worn clothes so tight over his muscles that she couldn't deny their presence. His face bore a lot less innocence too, though the boyish charm had metamorphosed into rugged handsomeness.

She pinched her hand to regain some good sense. His looks changed nothing. He'd still chased her, she'd still run, and both would keep doing so. He was a Clock of the Clocks of London – an old investigative family and the reason Michael had fallen in love with the business in the first place. Yet more proof of Michael's hand in this.

She reached for her work. Time was of the essence. During her flight from Michael's hired hand, she'd lost some of her drawings, but not ones of the boy. At least, not all of them. She chose the sheet with the image of the poor lad's hand. She noticed elements she hadn't picked up while drawing – her mind worked so strangely that way. When she drew, the image flew into her head, straight through her heart and out into the graphite pencil. Analysis came later.

Cuts.

Jagged marks, almost as if the boy had, barehanded, defended himself against a knife.

She swallowed and flipped the papers facedown while her stomach turned on itself. The gravity of it hit like a wave on the surface. She'd never seen a dead body before. In the tunnel, the boy had presented as a subject, something to draw and capture in form. Now the reality of it hit, twisting her insides into terrible knots. A dead child.

A baby really. She shivered as the papers fell from her hands.

She didn't want to be alone in this place.

She wanted her bed.

She wanted her mother.

She wanted home.

Her hands stretched to both ends of her shawl until she wrapped the edges tight around her and cried herself to a fitful sleep. Horrid images clawed into her dreams the whole wretched, lonely night.

The poor boy's face never strayed from memory, begging her for justice.

He'd get it. She woke tired, cold, hungry, but ferociously determined.

And not alone.

"Who...who..."

She couldn't get the rest of the sentence out as the form moved from shadows and into the glow of the scheduled morning lights.

The handsome man from yesterday twirled his hat and nodded. As before, he wore a black suit and large bowtie, both horribly out of fashion and yet wildly mystifying.

He put the hat on the desk and reached into his overcoat. "Miss?"

"You!" Moira rolled off the bed and grabbed the nearest weapon. The pencil would have to suffice. "How dare you enter my chambers!"

His eyes traced her movement and he smiled before pulling out a crushed bundle of folded papers. "I believe these are yours. You dropped them—"

"While I was being chased through the city. Who sent you? Drop the papers on the bed and leave. I'll have you arrested for this."

The man's face betrayed nothing. No surprise, but no guilt either. "No one sent me. Those are spectacular drawings. Did you—"

"My drawings are none of your concern. Why are you here if no one sent you? What kind of gentleman—"

"So you're being hunted and ran here. You don't belong in these tunnels. Your words and dress betray you."

"Neither do you, Mister..."

"Clock. Patrick Clock. And I'll wager I'm closer to these parts than you are. Why did you run?"

"Just as I suspected. I know who you are and who sent you. Don't pretend you don't know me."

"Michael's sister."

"I have a name."

"Miss Moira. Yes and no. No one sent me. Where's your family?"

"Preparing to kill you for walking into a woman's bedroom."

"Yes, but from where? They're not here. They wouldn't dream of putting you in a place like this."

"That's none of your concern, Mr. Clock."

"Well?"

"Well what?"

"Why did you run?"

"What else does one do when a madman chases her down the street like a common villain?"

"Madman? Madam, you're the one drawing pictures of—"

"It is part of my investigation."

His mouth twisted to a pucker.

She might have found it adorable had he not chased her last night and broken into her room this morning.

"What are you trailing? And you can put down your weapon. I'm not going to hurt you. Nor you me."

She raised it higher. "Missing children. Your turn."

"The same, in a manner of speaking."

"Me?"

"Don't be so conceited. And what did you learn at the scene?"

"Well..." She hesitated for the briefest of moments, then told and showed him everything. Let him run and tell Michael what a good job she'd done so far. "Notice the wounds on the hands and the direction of the blood droplets trailing away from the body."

"Do you have images of the crowd?"

"Yes, some. Well, one. Here." She spared him a glance before dropping the graphite weapon and picking up her stack. She waved him to the window and pointed out the people. "None appear suspicious."

"Good gracious. You've captured every emotion here. It's all on their faces."

His voiced carried a timbre of wonderment and she had to bite her lip to keep from smiling. It didn't work. She'd impressed him.

Yes!

This was it – the chance she'd waited for. She had a few failings, but being daft was not among them. Someone had managed to break into her room on her first night in London. If she proceeded with this, she'd undoubtedly run into enemies. Enemies who'd behave a lot less pleasantly upon finding her at night. Enemies not restrained by a friendship with her brother. "You need me, Mr. Clock."

"Sorry?"

"For this. My work. When we get to the scene of a crime—"

"We?"

"Yes. We. When we get there, you'll be busy investigating, while I can record the whole memory. The faces. The environment. You're right, I've captured everything in these images. Even that tiny face in the window. There, do you see it?"

"Good Lord! Was he there the whole time? We need to find that boy."

"We again? Sounds good," she said, which led to a very impressive round of swearing on his part. He made for the door, but she tapped a finger on his shoulder. "Mr. Clock, let us be plain. We haven't discussed the cost of my employment."

"I can compensate you for this information, but—"

"But you know I'm right. As we are on the same expedition, it is most expeditious that we work together. Of course, no one would hire a woman outright, but that is exactly why we need one another. Wouldn't you say, sir?"

"I wouldn't, Miss Gear."

"Moira Gear, Private Investigator. It sounds lovely, doesn't it? You're smiling. I can see you breaking."

He pointed to his face. "This? This is a grimace. And these are folded arms. Your brother will kill me. You must see how improper this is."

"He doesn't have to know. Besides, if you send me home, I'll come back, only I'll be alone and who will protect poor little me?" She shouldn't have laughed, but the man's face, his whole stance, had her cheeks quivering. "Look at that. Our first argument as business partners. We're smiling about it already. Twenty shillings a week."

"Five."

"Because the full payment has been amended in consideration of my room and board. Correct?"

"Your what?"

"I accept."

"Just a minute."

"We haven't got one. You're right, Patrick. May I call you Patrick?"

"No."

"Yes, but that boy may be in danger. We should leave immediately. I'll just grab my bag."

"But—"

"I'll be only a minute. I never really had a chance to unpack."

Chapter IV

She double-stepped to keep up with Mr. Clock's absurd pace. Now that she didn't have to bother about which angle was best to insert a pencil into his eyes, it left her free to fully examine him. "Attractive" was the word she'd have used, though not in the usual ways. He'd suffered a broken nose or three, and the hint of a scar created a little divot above his left eye. If she didn't know any better, she'd have labeled him a pugilist, but he was too smart for that and his clothes too fine.

"I'd be most appreciative if you kept up, Miss Gear."

And too rude and too well spoken. "Perhaps if you'd slow your monstrous gait down to a lope?"

"Am I a dog now?"

"Don't be ridiculous. Dogs wouldn't enter a stranger's bedroom. They know better."

Patrick stopped and pivoted. His chin fell to his chest. "Must I continuously apologize?"

"Once would be nice."

"I have."

"You haven't, but I don't hold grudges."

"You shouldn't, not when I'm paying the check." But amusement twinkled in his eye and her tummy did a most unwelcome roll at it. She didn't have time to fuss with gorgeous men. Much safer to concentrate on the city around her.

And what a city it was. It left her picking up her jaw every few steps. The first time she'd traveled this street, she'd been far too focused on finding shelter. Walking with Patrick, however, gave her opportunity to take in the horrid surroundings.

Lean-to houses rested against older, dilapidated buildings. Its occupants held out beggars' cups and she stopped to reach into her pocket. Patrick's hand locked onto hers. "No."

"But..."

The grip tightened and he half yanked, half dragged her down the street. "Look around you, Miss Gear. It isn't safe here."

"I managed."

"You wouldn't have lasted another day. Listen, London doesn't care about you or these people. Have you seen any emergency evacuation signs? Any escape tunnels or transport subs here?"

"I...well...I hadn't noticed."

"You haven't. Too right. It's a desperate area with desperate people. We've lived in these tunnels for hundreds of years. They were meant to be a new Eden. Built for the chosen few when the waves took back the land. Now what? That talk of equality and community has gone to rot."

"All the more reason to help where we can."

"Help starts at the steps of Parliament. You hand out currency here and they'll damn near crack your neck and the tunnels to get more out of you. We'd never make it back. It'll be this way until the waters recede once again."

She shivered and drew her shawl tight around her. It was the old tale that mothers used to scare their children into good behavior. That people lived under the waters as they were meant to, but eventually moved to land. And then as centuries passed, terrible centuries, they forgot their watery beginnings. As before, as the ever-cycle continued, the waters rose again, the cities were swallowed and people rebuilt the tunnels of legend and moved back to the sea. If the stories held true, they were less than five generations from the cycle starting anew. Fingers suddenly quite frozen, she crossed her arms and tried to convince herself that there must be a temperature malfunction down here.

"Silence now? Have I frightened you, girl? Good."

That put some much-needed life back in her. She got her bearings and squared her shoulders. "Moira. Or Ms. Gear. 'Girl' won't suffice, Patrick."

He bowed, circling his arms. "Sincerest apologies, milady. This way."

"Your sarcasm is duly noted."

She entered the dilapidated building ahead of him. Broken and crushed children's toys lay strewn on the floor. She stepped on a loose board and would have slid, save for Mr. Clock's arm holding her steady. Their shuffling steps were the only sounds coming from inside the dark, soulless building.

"The boy was in the second window on the right, second floor, correct?"

"Yes."

"I want you to draw this. This room and everything in it. I'll find the boy. Scream if anyone comes near." He pressed a small folding knife into her hand. "Don't be afraid to use this."

"Let's hope I can return it to you unblemished."

"You keep that. Now draw." He tapped the paper, then disappeared up the stair.

Despite her bravado, she strained to hear his boots for as long as possible. The place had a heaviness about it that bordered on smothering. There wasn't much light or any best location, but she folded her gloves inside out, brushed herself a somewhat clean space on the floor and drew.

Time fell away as it did every time she put graphite in her hands. Graphite, such an extravagance, but it moved across the paper with the elegance that only this rare product could create. Even its sound, its scratching, may well have been the clearest of sea bells.

Had an hour passed? Or five minutes? She didn't know and didn't care when she set about her work. No surprise then that she jumped and screamed at the hand on her shoulder. "Patrick! Sorry, Mr. Clock."

"Patrick's fine, but now I know that you can't be left alone."

"I..."

"It's fine. There's no boy, but I see fingerprints in the dust on the window. I need you to draw that room. Can you do it?"

She did. She drew until her fingers ached and her back twinged in pain. It was Patrick who again pulled her out of it, concern etched across his face. "Where do go when you draw?"

"Nowhere. My mind simply focuses on each line, every angle and shadow." She squinted and rubbed her eyes with her thumb and forefinger, holding out her tools of trade to Patrick with the other hand. "I get headaches sometimes. Eyestrain, my doctor says."

Patrick's warm hand guided her out, providing nearly as much comfort as being outside itself. "You've done more than enough. Let's go home and compare my notes to your work."

She squinted against the day outside, wishing the afternoon lighting schedule to speed up for once, allowing the natural sunlight to bathe them in blessed dimness.

A city wagon trilled its arrival. Patrick waved for the drivers to stop their pedaling and guided her to a sectioned-off part of the green-draped vehicle. She took a window seat and leaned out the side, watching the streets morph into the sectioned-off pebble-paths to which she was more accustomed.

She took a deep breath and, within a few minutes of the slow, rolling pace, leaned back in the cushioned sheet. Even the air was cleaner here – almost as if this set of tunnels ran on its own filtration system. Crisp too. "The humidity is different here."

"Everything is different for us. Isn't it the same where you're from? The richer areas hire the best hydro-engineers to retrobuild the area, well above city standards. Never mind the basics. The upper roofs are cleaned three times a week, outside and in. There are new tunnel hubs under construction, ones deeper than thirty meters, where people are willing to sacrifice natural light for timed artificial glow year round. By invitation, of course."

"But surely the city won't allow that to happen?"

"Why not? We're overpopulated. If we can't count on a good plague to help thin us out, then we'll have to wait for the continued degradation of—"

"How could you say such a thing?"

Patrick leaned over to ring the bell and helped her stand as the wagon pedals rolled to a stop. He donned his hat, paid the driver and held out his arm, muscled and strong. "Have you heard of a man named Darwin?"

She shook her head.

"He lived back in the second 1800s...I think. Maybe the third. He theorized that only those able to adapt would survive."

"Like the people who still live on land?"

Patrick tipped his hat as they passed a gaggle of old biddies. Each and every one of them stared her down, but he didn't stop, nor did he otherwise address them. "You and I both know that's a temporary thing. The water will take that over too."

"You sound as bad as my father."

"But it's true, Moira. Water owns the world."

"Arabia used to be a desert."

He snorted and turned her down a side street to a lane of midsized row houses. "Well, it's not now, is it? We get agents stuffing their green brochures in our postboxes once a month. I'd take blue to green any day, thank you very much."

"Afraid of a little land, are we, Patrick?"

He stopped so fast that it made the gravel beneath *her* feet skid. She "oomphed," and he smiled as he turned to face her head on. One massive hand planted itself on her shoulder while the other shook a reprimanding index finger in her face. "I have faced the most terrible of humanity. I have solved crimes so despicable that they make the constables cry. Patrick Clock, Esquire, is not afraid of desolate land miles away from a decent shore, Miss

Moira Gear. There's but one thing that keeps me shivering in fear at night. If you ask very nicely, I'll tell you."

She leaned in, unsuccessful in biting back her grin. "And that is?"

"Tiny women with deadly pencils."

"Oh, you!" She *thwaped* him on the shoulder and immediately followed it with an apology. One he laughingly did not accept.

He did, however, open the gate to a tri-level home, about the width of two standard row houses. It was the largest on the street, though not the fanciest. Gold windows popped against blue paint that could use another coat or two. She also lamented the lack of a grass lawn, though the pebbles were well placed and a few potted plants strained towards solar shields above. It definitely needed a woman's touch.

"This is where we'll live and work. You can exit all you like, but try not to enter on your own."

"That makes no sense."

"Trust me on this. Now, you have full access to every area here, save my office and the attic. That belongs to Kennerick."

"Another houseguest?"

Patrick looked up, then down and dropped his hands to his hips. "You could call him that."

"What would you call him?"

"An annoying, self-involved, overconfident prat. And my foster brother."

"Patrick, I was never grammarian, but I do wonder if that is irony or situational coincidence."

"You're quick."

"Quite." The exchange earned another smile. In the space of just two days, she'd gone from heartbreak to wonder to horror and now this – gainfully and happily employed. She crossed the threshold into a home of burgundy-carpeted floors and lights running along the top edges, not too dissimilar from those used in the better class of submarines. Light poured in through the open windows and onto yellow and gold furniture. "This is not the color palette I would have expected. Not that I'm judging."

"My grandmother's tastes. She was a grand woman. I find neither the inclination nor time to rid myself of it." Heavy footfalls on the stairs had Patrick nodding in that direction. "My apologies."

"For?"

But he'd turned away to address the...dear heavens...nearly naked man. "Kennerick, would you like to put some clothes on?"

She turned away, but gracious, it hurt to do so. The man was ferociously gorgeous, almost as much as Patrick, but in a completely different way. He looked to be from the Italian waters, with blue eyes and dark brown hair slicked back and gathered at his nape. Suspenders hung down at his sides, and he wasn't alone. The click-clack of running feet surely belonged to the woman with the half-laced dress as she scuttled by, breasts heaving. Well, that was an experience.

"Is this our new serving girl? She's cute. I'll pay you double to serve me in a more delicious—"

"Miss Moira Gear is going to assist in this latest case."

"Assist? Miss?"

She did glance up then, and Kennerick did what she supposed was to have passed for dressing. He slipped his suspenders over his shoulders and buttoned his trousers. His gaze alternated between his working hands and her face. "You're having a go, Patrick."

"He is not. We're investigating the same set of missing persons. It makes the most sense to work together. Are you an investigator too, Mr. Kennerick?"

"Doctor Kennerick Clock." And with that, the man whirled around to face Patrick. "What is this?"

"Just what she says."

Well, she wouldn't be talked around. "I am in the room. If you have a question, you can address me directly."

He didn't. "Why is she here? How is it that you get to bring yours home anytime you like?"

"She's not...Kennerick!"

The physician shot her a glance over his shoulder. "Not that I don't understand, she'll be good for...wait. You're serious." The swarthy man turned to stand shoulder to shoulder with Patrick. "You don't look like a Moira."

"You don't look like a Clock."

Patrick chuckled. Doctor Kennerick pouted. Not exactly forward progress.

"Matron Clock wouldn't have stood for this," Kennerick added with a lot less flair.

"Yeah, well, she isn't here anymore. And despite whatever you're thinking, Moira's got a rare talent."

"Has she?" Kennerick shot her a lecherous wink.

What had she gotten herself into? She'd prepared herself to be bold but accidently veered into the foolish along the way. Madness, more precisely. A single woman with one man was scandalous enough, but two?

Perhaps if she left now...

But no. For so many reasons, no.

More, she had no protection. The murderers and kidnappers she hunted wouldn't think twice about making her disappear. For better or for worse, the die was cast. She curled her lips into a sneer. "I draw."

"You draw? You draw!?! So? I refuse to believe this."

"More than that, Kennerick. She captures everything as it was, never missing a detail. An invaluable asset."

"I'm not doubting her assets," Kennerick said in a tone that less than thrilled. "But she won't get our afternoon tea?"

"No."

"And she will not cook?"

"No," Patrick answered again. "She will, however, help us save lives, if that's all right with you."

"She can't cook while she does it?"

"Gentlemen, I've had enough of being talked about, talking around and talked over. If you can't behave enough to address me *while* dressed, then please be on your way, Mr. Kennerick. Patrick, I'd like to see my room now. I could do for a rest."

"She calls you Patrick? And am I being given 'the what for' in my home?"

"Kennerick, I believe you are." Patrick held out his arm with a quick "ma'am" and led her up the stairs. Her bravado, thrilling though it was, didn't remove one massive thing – the very fact that she was being led up the stairs by a man.

She patted her purse, the side that held the knife he'd given her, but somehow knew she wouldn't need it. This was THE Patrick Clock. He'd protect her. His comrade, on the other hand, left a little more to be desired. She opened her mouth to ask more of the doctor, but coherent speech gave way to gap-mouthed wonderment at what happened next.

Halfway up the stair, Patrick lifted a bronze lever concealed between two balusters. He prodded her back a few steps as a section of the stairs lifted up, revealing a hidden room below.

Kennerick's voice popped up on her left. "If you tell anyone about this, I'll have to kill you. Which begs the question, Patrick. Why are we showing her this?"

"Because she won't say a word," Patrick answered through clenched teeth.

"You know this, how?"

She faced Kennerick head on, refusing to let him talk around her again. "Because my word means something. Honor may not be something you're accustomed to, but some of us still have it. And if I judge Patrick correctly, this is his subtle way of letting me know that the house is full of trickery and I could easily disappear in it."

"So then why are you here? I ask a second time. You talk like a lady, yet you stroll into the home of—"

"I have to solve these crimes. Children are disappearing—"

"We're not investigating children," Kennerick fired back.

Patrick stepped between them, holding out the drawing papers he still carried for her. Kennerick snatched them away and held them to the light. "Oh. I see. Eidetic memory coupled with artistic ability." He looked at her, top to bottom, and handed her the drawings. "Stay away from the attic."

"I've been told."

And with that, the odd man turned away, heading back downstairs. "One last thing. I'll keep your secret, but unless you intend to move about under the cover of darkness, Mrs. Huxton will be up in arms about this. Never mind the girl's family. Well played, Patrick. You've ruined the woman without even touching her."

"Out!"

"I'm done, brother. Ma'am."

As much as she hated the man, he was right. The only solace came in knowing that she was right too.

"Well. That's Kennerick. He's a bit to take."

"He's also not a fool," she finished for him. "I know what I'm getting into."

"We'll tell people that you're family. We won't use your real name, either. So I'm clear, why aren't I contacting Michael again? Please, make the reason better than last time."

"Because I'm disowned."

"Liar. You ran away. Why?"

"Because I have more to offer than a face. I can help where no one else is willing. Have you never had a cause worth fighting for, Patrick? Your grandmother is legendary, but shouldn't we live in a London where she wasn't the best *female* investigator but the best investigator, full stop? That's the London I want."

"Society has rules, Miss Gear."

"I'm living under your roof. Call me Moira and we shall change them."

"The rules?"

"Society."

Indecision marred his face as surely as if she'd drawn it there herself. In a way, she had. Patrick glanced toward a painting of the famous, stone-faced Matron Clock before turning back to her. "This way. This is where we'll work."

With the stairs now firmly up in the air, they walked down a secondary set of steps beneath them into a large room stacked with shelves, a desk and several tables. "Here's where I keep the evidence I gather. For security's sake, I hold on to everything until I turn in the culprit to the authorities. Better that way. Don't come down here without permission."

"I understand. Um, who is Mrs. Huxton? Your intended? I shouldn't wish to cause her distress." He blinked at the catch in her voice and she could have kicked herself for it. She hadn't *meant* for it to happen. Why should she care? She didn't. Really. Simply a matter of propriety. Right?

"An old biddy across the street. She does nothing all day but stare out her window while pretending not to stare out her window. Then she spends Friday running around, reporting what she's seen."

"That's annoying." But an odd relief washed over her. She hadn't liked the idea of him attached.

"Yes, but she has her uses. Every so often we'll get someone sniffing around. They don't go undetected with Huxton on the watch. She's a rather cheap first layer of defense. Head still hurt?"

"What? Yes, a bit."

He nodded and led her out the way they came. After lowering the steps, they climbed up to the next flight of the above stairs. From the guardrail, she caught a glimpse of a scowling Kennerick passing from one side of the house to the other, teacup and kettle in hand.

Patrick cleared his throat. "I'll be just up the hall from you. Kennerick is down the other direction. If you need anything, knock. Every other day, Mrs. Catherine is our femme de chamber. Don't expect much. She comes to do a bit of light cleaning in the public areas. You'll be responsible for your own mess, but she'll cook extras that even I can reheat. Any pressing you need, she'll do that too. Breakfast at eight, then?"

"Thank you."

"Don't thank me yet." Then he bowed and walked away.

She'd have appreciated the help of Mrs. Catherine right now, but on her own she managed to sort out the lighting and move the arm-sagging white sheets from the bed, table and dresser. Each sent up waves of dust, but the window was too heavy to open and she was too tired to try more than once. Without a single additional look around the room, she unlaced her shoes, stripped to her underlooms and crawled beneath the inviting blankets of the Clock Estate.

Patrick stalked back down from Moira's doorway, ready for battle. He couldn't avoid it, but the thought had occurred to go to bed and delay it. He'd been on his feet all day – he deserved the rest. Knowing Ken, though, the fool would burst down his door to discuss it.

"I thought we were similarly burdened with an overabundance of intelligence."

He followed Ken's voice into the drawing room, feet dragging. He walked right by the occupied chair to the plate of cold cuts on the table. "You saw what she can do."

"How is it appropriate for you to bring a stranger into my house—"

"Our."

"Our house without asking first? Matron Clock left this to both of us. The business and house and the money, and yet—"

"You spend the money and I manage the business. That's how it goes, isn't it brother?"

"Not fair."

He dipped his head in acquiescence and took a seat. Rascal and womanizer though he was, Kennerick had always done his share. Somewhat. Well, a solid forty-five percent of the time. On more fingers than he could count, he'd found Ken bent over a corpse on the examination table or giving medical testimony. Never mind taking over when the reading addled his head overmuch. Still... "You won't notice her."

"Is that a hope or a request? I stand by what I said earlier. You've never brought one home. Whiskey in your tea?"

"Please. And she was in rather dire straits."

"As are most of the people we come across. About her assets, her drawings I mean, if she's earning her keep with you, she needs to do the same for me. I may need her in the lab."

"Done."

"You speak for her?"

"Consider it an apology."

"And her reputation?"

"You care?"

"Point. No. But you're the type who would."

True enough and he did. But he needed her, too. Such a talent on the right case could bring in a much needed influx of money.

Oh, who was he lying to?

It was the ringing of Matron's voice in his ear. How many times had the Grand Dame defied expectations? Wouldn't she support such a woman herself? "I have an obligation to look after her."

"Based on?"

"Her brother. We go back."

"He knows she's here, then?"

When he didn't meet Kennerick's eyes, the arse snorted and choked on this liquor. "You're breaking the pact, aren't you?"

"Say it again and I'll box your ears."

"It's all right. I forgive you. Better you than me."

"To be clear, brother, if I were to marry, the money would be mine. You'd still have to claim your own bride and portion of the estate."

"So you have thought about it?"

"No." Yes. Possibly. Only in passing. He tried to blot out that small snippet of memory in regards to Matron. A tiny clause in her will that left them struggling at times. "I understand her now. She'd have known that we'd marry at some point. Her will was all to speed it up."

Kennerick downed his drink and went for another. "That old woman's still besting us from the grave."

That was how they'd seen it. One final gloat from the glorious lady. And, just as when they were children, they'd plotted to sidestep the rules.

Matron had more than a passing touch of madness in her genius. She'd withheld the full sum of their inheritance until two conditions were met: they'd reached the age of twenty-three and they were married.

The former stipulation ensured they didn't rest on *her* laurels. The latter, well, she'd deemed it a way of keeping them human. She'd warned that her profession had kept her from the love of her life, and she wouldn't have it stand in the way for her boys.

"I miss Grandma."

"Is that why the girl's here?"

"For the dozenth time, no."

Kennerick ran splayed hands across his face and leaned forward. "We need repairs. We pay Catherine too much. There's equipment and bribery and all those tiny things that add up."

"What are you suggesting?" But he knew already. They weren't poor, but they needed breathing room. A marriage would grant it. "I've only just met her. Met her again, that is."

"And yet she's in our house."

"Does it always come back to that?"

"How could it not?"

They retreated to their corners for a moment, shoving in food and throwing darts with their eyes. Kennerick caved first with a grin. "Apology accepted, but the second she no longer works, she's out on her plump bum."

"Fine. Now, tell me, who was that young lady flying down the stairs upon our arrival?"

"Young? Lady? You're being awful generous on both accounts. She's a tart out on her husband."

"You sound so remorseful."

"Keep your sarcasm. There's nothing to be remorseful about – she's good at what she does. Bless her."

Chapter V

Moira arrived downstairs at 7:58 the next morning in a plain brown dress that did nothing to mar her beauty.

Catherine gasped at her arrival but quickly recovered with a curtsey and pulled out the chair. The women had to be about the same age, but Mrs. Catherine had a motherly quality about her. Having a half dozen kids in rapid succession did that to a woman, he supposed.

The difference in their experiences piddled about his brain. Two women, one privileged and on a grand adventure. The other, married since fourteen and already bent and haggard at twenty-two. From here out, their paths would only continue to diverge.

"Miss Moira, this is Catherine. She'll see to anything you need."

Moira could have ignored her or talked down to the aproned servant. Instead, she smiled graciously and even went so far as to hold out her hand. Catherine gasped, giggled and curtsied, looking for the first time as young as her true age.

Kennerick rolled his eyes but otherwise kept quiet as the piping-hot foods were brought to the small circular table. After all the sausages were laid and the trio alone, Moira spoke up.

"The bedroom was beautiful. Thank you. And Doctor, I apologize for my behavior last night. I imagine me arriving in your home came as an unexpected shock."

"At least someone has some manners around here," Kennerick mumbled, eyes still locked on his food.

"I think she's expecting something a little more gracious in response, brother."

"Perhaps we should focus on the merits of our cases," Moira interrupted, planting a stack of sheets on the table between the cream and butter.

Kennerick snatched up the top sheets. "Cases? I thought you were working on the same issue?"

"No. I'm investigating the children. He's looking for a child."

"Not exactly. I'm looking for a man-child still suckling off daddy's teat. Man's name is McCoy. I did some footwork while you two slept. He's out running up charges on his father's signature for clothes, wine and the like. Never at places where his father's face is known, however. Each and every establishment, at least that I've encountered, is a business of the nouveau riche. I'll attest to not knowing how this case intersects with that of the missing ragamuffins—"

"Children. They are called children, Patrick. I've made a chart; perhaps you can send it around, Kennerick?"

"Huh?" He looked up from her hand-drawn papers, eyes unfocused. "The chart is good...I suppose."

Patrick took the expertly lined map and the colorful dots splattered across the city. "Each dot is a subject?"

"Child. Each dot represents a once living, breathing child. Red is a dead child. Green indicates a missing child. Hash marks indicate they are older than ten."

Then by her reckoning, most were far younger than that and all in the tunnels near their investigations yesterday. Moira was right. "How could something this big go unnoticed?"

"It's like you said, Patrick. No one cares about those tunnels or the so-called ragamuffins that live there. I also agree with Doctor Kennerick that these cases are separate. But it doesn't mean we can't work together on both of them ."

His case felt very small and insignificant all of a sudden. He chased money. She chased justice. A fair difference between the two.

Kennerick shot them the same look. "My guest, the fascinating girl you met yesterday, complained about theft on the rise among the upper-lipped. It's not in the news, of course. Shame, you see, but she'd mentioned it more than once. Several robberies, and they blame King Hellion's gang."

"Who?"

"Hellion," Patrick answered Moira. "The man changes, but the name stays the same. He's rumored to run an army of pickpockets. Though that's a little different than what your lady suggested," he said, turning to his brother.

"True. But if we consider crime a business, the nature of a business is to grow and expand."

"Which means," Moira interrupted, "that this Hellion person needs more pickpockets."

"So we're connecting the cases now? All this conjecture isn't moving us in the right direction. Moira, stick with the children from the poorer tunnels. Kennerick, I want you to follow up on the thefts."

"I'll do my level best to pry it out of my female friends."

"I'm sure that you will. I'll finish up with the McCoy mess. The sooner I close that case, the sooner I can move on to the other two."

"I rather think the children take precedence."

"I'm sure you do, Moira. But McCoy pays handsomely. This isn't a business run on charity. This house, your salary. It all needs to be paid for."

"Salary!?"

But she dismissed Kennerick's outburst with a wave. "Then I'll work for free."

"Then so shall I. Would you like to be the one to tell Mrs. Catherine that her services will no longer be needed? That on the interest of saving children, hers will starve?"

"Well...no."

"Good. McCoy's boy will buy us time to save those children. Justice is fine, but not to the exclusion of reality. We can't afford to work for free. Kennerick, in your indulgences, learn to pass along our calling card."

"A step ahead of you. I have an afternoon appointment tomorrow with a Lord Confid. His wife found our advert in the dailies and he needs hush-hush service."

"Did we put an advert out this month?"

"Not exactly. I perhaps misspoke. Though I did meet his wife. She's been generously blessed with a huge—"

"Kennerick!"

"A huge heart," the man finished with a smile.

"Right. Well, until then, I want you with Moira out investing these dots, eh, children on her map. She draws, you talk to people. Then follow up with your Confid connection. I'll work the kidnapping front and see what the police can give me about Hellion. Maybe those badges know something they're not sharing. We'll meet up later to discuss."

Kennerick drifted away, but how could she leave this room? Here, in the very center of investigative work and she was a part of it. "Do you mind if we spend some time downstairs, Patrick? I noticed dailies down there and thought perhaps another look was in order."

"Questioning my genius?"

She gasped and fluttered her eyes, dragging the back of her hand to her mouth in mock horror. "Perish the thought."

He mirrored her ridiculous face and held out an arm, leading her first up and then down to the secret room. Soft lighting met them, and the faint scent of seaweed tea seemed infused into the very walls. She ran her hands along the tables and eyed his desk. "I'm of half a mind to demand a desk of my own down here."

"I'm of half a mind to give you one," he said, no small amount of self-disgust in his voice. He scooted a chair on the opposite side of it and motioned for her to take a seat before sliding into his own. "Here's what I have so far."

One hour in and they were hunched over forehead to forehead, reviewing possibilities of Hellion's involvement in any of the cases.

Two hours in and he'd moved her chair to his side of the table...and directly next to him. All in the interest of better seeing things at the same time, of course.

Her arm brushed against his a few times.

His arm brushed against hers a few times more. "Sorry, I—"

"If you apologize again, Patrick, I'll take that as your subtle way of informing me that my arm is so offensive that you wish to remind me to keep it away."

He lifted her left arm by the wrist, sniffed it and winced, sticking out his tongue. "Disgusting."

"Oh, I will throttle you." And darn her, she tried.

He fended off her laughter-filled attacks with gentle pushes until the kettle whistled and he pulled back, shaking his head. "Look at us, like children. I should get that tea, though I find myself with a sudden dislike for the stuff."

Back still turned, he froze as if he wished he'd never said it. Never mind the dizzying delight it gave her that he had. He liked her and that was very well and good because...well...perhaps she liked him too.

"I've decided tea is rather rude, Patrick. Don't you think? Always barging into conversations."

The tense back relaxed and when Patrick turned around with teacups in hand, a soft and not-so-regretful smile lingering on his lips. "Perhaps it was reminding us to behave."

"I have found in my journey here that sometimes it's best not to. Can you imagine how boring I'd be if I'd behaved?" she asked, taking a cup from his hand.

"Or worse, how bored I'd be." He shivered and blew across the rim, sending tendrils of steam into the air. "I'll have you know that I'm not accustomed to bringing strange women into my home."

"Am I strange?"

"A very curious specimen indeed."

"Specimen? Am I to be studied?"

He tapped his finger against his chin. "Never seen such a creature before. Lovely, but with strange habits."

She pointed to the ceiling. "And in an even stranger habitat, must I remind you."

"True. I commend you for being a part of it."

"Honestly Patrick, there's not a single place I'd rather be."

"I think..." He grabbed her hand, apologized and let go.

She grabbed his right back and held on. "You think what?"

He brought their entwined fingers to his mouth and laid a quick kiss across her knuckles. "I think you should go on up to your room, Moira, before I forget to be the gentleman my grandmother raised me to be."

Chapter VI

An hour later, Moira met Kennerick downstairs. She steeled her nerves, preparing for it to come, but instead of hooting or shouting at her appearance, he'd removed his cap and put it on her head, pulling the peak of it down past her brow. He took her short, pressed hair and stuffed it up into the crown.

"Better," was all he'd said of her dressing up as a boy and stepped out the door.

She took that as approval and smiled into her brother's old short jacket from school, stolen from her mother's memory chest. A thief in her own household.

"Don't dawdle."

"I'm not. So you and Patrick are...uh, brothers?"

"Raised by the same woman."

"Matron Clock?"

"You have a lot of questions."

"That's my job."

"Temporarily. Over my left shoulder, what do you see?"

"A house."

Kennerick's cough sounded too much like a laugh for her liking. He squatted and redid his laces. "Top floor, far left window. Don't be obvious. Point to something above."

She did. She could just make out what she *thought* to be a school of jellyfish, but at this impossible distance, it could be the ephemera of her mind. What she hadn't missed was the bundle of white hair staring back from the house across the way. "Is that the infamous Mrs. Huxton?"

"He's filled you in on the particulars, then? You can't let her see you. Not as a woman, anyway." Then he jumped up smiling and pointed to his boot. "Shine my shoes."

"I will not."

"You will. You're the new houseboy."

"Whose idea was this?"

"I'm pointing, milady. The longer I do, the more ol' Huxton will wonder what the matter is. Don't make me have to box your ears."

"You wouldn't dare."

"I'd do anything to protect your honor."

She would have loved to smack the smirk right off his face, but instead, she dropped to her knees and wiped the heel of her palm against the toe of his boot. She ought to have spit on it, but it would hurt her more than him, and despite all of this, she was still a lady. "Is it working? Is she gone?"

"Yes and of course not. This is the most excitement she's had all week."

Moira stood and jammed her heel into the newly cleaned boot. Kennerick's resulting grunt mollified her somewhat, but she kept her head down like a good little houseboy and backed away.

"Right." He took his bicycle from the latch, leaving the much larger one behind. The other was Patrick's, she presumed, but even with modifications, it'd be too large for either of them. Kennerick pushed his alongside them as they walked. After a length, he stopped at a small meatpie stand several streets away. Its owner, with a mustache as grand as any cycle's handlebars, smiled, and for the first time, Kennerick seemed almost human and smiled back before easing into congenial conversation with the man.

A small boy rushed up to her, tugging at her pants legs. "You new?"

Unsure of her best masculine voice, she bobbed her head.

"You mute?"

Another head bob.

"You wi' him?"

And a third.

"Good. I stick wi' me Pa. Lads without Pas are getting nicked around here. Is he on the case?" The boy beamed at her response and let out a yip of air. "Good. Now that the Clocks is on it, the person will stop stealing them boys. Doc Clock comes back every day, same time. You can tell the clock by the Clock, me Pa says."

The mustachioed man called his son over and Kennerick waved them goodbye. He rustled the lad's hair when he passed.

"You deign to lower yourself—"

"I value people who prove their worth, Miss Gear. Something you've yet to do entirely. Now, in your portraiture of the dead boy, his eyes were open. Is the same in the other cases?"

She shrugged. "Could it mean something?"

"Everything."

He turned left when he ought to have turned right. She didn't bring it up until the bells and claxons of the hub's center came to earshot. "We're going in the wrong direction."

"No we're not."

"But—"

"Any good investigator knows to follow the lead where it takes them. This lead brings us here, the coroner's office."

It was one thing to stumble upon the scene of a crime and draw. It was something else entirely to walk into a building of death, surrounded by death, asking questions of, well, death. "They won't let us in."

"I'm a doctor."

"They won't let me in."

"You're my assistant."

"I won't go in."

"Ahh. I promise, any children in there won't hurt you."

"That isn't funny, Kennerick."

"Oh, we've advanced to first names, have we? Fine, Moira," he said, spitting out her name like it burned his tongue to say it. "If you want to play a man's game, be prepared for the rough of it. We need paperwork. That's it. Ladies first," he added through pearly, clenched teeth.

He'd pushed her inside so fast that she hadn't had time to prepare for what waited within.

Corpses laid out amongst the papers?

Teeth hanging from ceilings?

She wiped damp hands against her pants and readjusted her hat, all the while keeping her eyes on the floor.

A floor she could almost describe as pleasant. Soft blue tiles with green waves on the edges. It didn't fit. Nor did the proprietor. The coroner was a small, cheery man with a bald head, round nose and dimpled, ruddy cheeks. He scared her more than the floor and corpses. Who could be happy here? He refused to grant them access to the paperwork but rattled off information at a ten-pound note and Kennerick's assertion that "a certain local lord inquired after his bastard son."

The man took a kerchief to his head before locking pudgy hands around his waist. "A few boys, all from the streets by the looks of them."

"And what of their pupils? Signs of mydriasis?"

"Yes, in about all of them. I'm not surprised. Belladonna, nightshade, mandrake – it's coming in from the upside. Never trust people who live on land, I'll tell you that much. Filling our streets with the drugs and such."

"But no evidence?" She coughed when the man's head jerked in her direction and lowered her voice. "No evidence of a young man, about nine? Red hair? That's what the lord's by-blow looked like."

Kennerick's eyebrows shot up as if suddenly remembering the conjured reason for their visit. Had she proven her worth yet?

His look was a grudging *yes*.

"No. No gingers," he said, rolling the note between his fingers. She caught the corner's glistening eye and the man shoved it into his pocket. "Anything else? No?"

"Actually—"

But he cut Kennerick right off. "I'll show you out."

A half breath later, they were free of the death house and trudging down the main streets of the tunnel. "Good recovery on your part, Moira."

"I know."

"No one likes a braggart."

"Who's bragging? So, there's an epidemic of intoxicants."

"Maybe, but it's immaterial to our case. He received the boys days after their deaths. Dilated pupils by chemical cause would have long passed. That boy in your drawing had blown pupils. Besides, that man's not trustworthy."

"He's the city coroner."

"The man said belladonna and nightshade."

"So?"

"Belladonna *is* nightshade. We can trust the facts, not his suppositions or analysis."

"Fine. Then we have seventeen boys from the slums with blown pupils."

"I need a body."

"They'll have been shuttled out into the seas already. All except the last, and we can't go back without rousing suspicion."

"Then we'll have to beat the police when the next one springs up."

"You're assuming there will be."

"At this rate, I expect many more." Kennerick led her across a busy intersection to a small bicycle shop at the apex of three tunnels. He held the side of his hand to her hip and kept it extended to just that height as if in measurement. "Wait here," he said, and then walked into the store.

With nothing else to do, she did, taking in the bright bustles, bowler hats and skipping children that painted the streets. Was this the life of an investigator? Pushed aside? Ignored?

No.

She needed to do more. Playing the part of a houseboy hadn't advanced her cause one bit. She needed to be free to speak openly, without concerns of giving herself away. Next time, she wouldn't be hampered by her gender. She'd use it. Somehow she'd find a way to be herself. Investigator. Female. Moira.

Kennerick came out with a green bicycle, complete with a ribboned basket.

"What's this?"

"Yours."

"It's lovely. I don't know how to thank you."

"Don't. I got tired of walking and it's coming out of your next three paychecks." He hopped onto his bicycle. "Your map. You lead. Where to first?"

The damned McCoy brat moved like a phantom. Patrick found himself always three steps behind young Samuel. Every description matched and yet no one knew more about him. This looked less like a wayward son and more like a mastermind on the run. Every step had been protected and guarded under several layers. Samuel had gone to each establishment at its busiest hour. He went to their newest workers and walked out with goods and money just under the threshold of questioning second glances.

It was a little too practiced for a spoiled lord. Perhaps he was under the control of nefarious hands. Then who did that leave as a suspect? No one requested ransom. No one left a note. The boy had nothing of value to offer, so why keep him? For this? A few clothes, wine and credits? It wasn't worth the hassle.

No. The boy must have left willingly and he must have *joined* some criminal enterprise.

The dailies lay strewn out on the table. Patrick would have to go through their articles with fresh eyes – this time not looking for evidence of McCoy but of an agency of crime so foolhardy to think taking him on was a good idea.

He cracked his neck, shoved a kelp chip in his mouth and started reviewing the news articles with fresh, if throbbing, eyes. As part of Greater London, there were five well-known criminal syndicates, each in one of the major hubs. Sure, someone might take a sub from Brighton to Margate to start a fuss, but that almost never happened. Each group held its claim with murderous possessiveness. Even Hellion.

He'd long wondered how a crook with children for partners managed to hold down this massive an area. The going assumption was a minor agreement with the local badges. They'd leave Hellion alone for small pickpocketing and together they'd work to keep out the heavies.

Mayhap Hellion was branching out.

Or someone was moving in.

All of this provided great job security for himself, no doubt about it, but for the young of London at risk, this – whatever it was – had to be stopped right now.

And yet, this wasn't his case. Not properly. It rested in the lap of his beautiful protégé. His lips twitched, imagining her face if he dared use that word in her presence.

The kettle whistled its reward and he went to pour himself a cup of tea. It took a lot longer for it come to a boil against the heating coils and pipes down here, but it was a fat lot better than trudging up and down the stairs to the small kitchen. He took the quiet moment of tea and chips for what it was and lay back in the heavy chair, letting his mind wander.

To her.

Again.

Ken was right, of course. Matron would not have approved of this. But she'd have approved of her. And of his motives. They were pure.

Mostly.

Honestly, he couldn't have left an innocent woman out there alone and on the streets. She wouldn't have lasted a day. Maybe a month on long odds.

Add to that, she was the type of woman who needed people around her. That he could relate to. No, this *had* been the gentlemanly thing to do. His goodwill had nothing at all to do with her pouty lips or wide eyes.

Or that waist that he'd love to wrap his arms around.

She was the type of woman a man held onto. Him, specifically. By what impossible odds could a woman so beautiful and so bright have landed on his doorstep? He had female companionship often enough, but to a have a women exercise his mind as well as his body would be an altogether new experience.

A delightful one.

But Moira wasn't a companion. She filled the bill as a proper lady. The kind men married, and he did *need* to marry.

Such a union would work. Or could have, had he not brought her into the fold. Talking to her of anything outside of work after promising her safe sanctuary made him a right and proper bastard of the worst order. He'd botched the whole thing now.

Bloody hell. He shook his head and exchanged his tea for something stronger. None of it helped clear his head of her. He didn't have time for this.

Best think of something else. Not work, not Moira.

He retreated to the safety of his childhood, scanning the papers for unsolved anagrams on back pages. Putting things in order. Finding truth. Yes, there was shelter there. Logic. Order. Reason.

Footsteps stomping above jerked him from that temporary sanctuary. A portion of the ceiling lifted for Moira and Kennerick to step through. "Well?"

"Good day to you too. I'll leave it to Doctor Kennerick to go first. His house, his right," Moira said with a little too much snap in her voice.

"She's rude, but right. She's been rude all day."

"And still here," she interrupted.

"We're both aware. Go on Kennerick."

"All the deaths are connected, at least medically speaking. There's nothing to tie this to the disappearances or your McCoy case. At least not yet. It occurred to me that we may be looking for someone in the medical profession. The results were too consistent."

"I'd hold back on that, Ken. For now, we just know they are done by the same person."

"But—"

"You could teach me or Moira how to do something. A medical something. That doesn't make us doctors."

"No. Quite. And there was nothing from the interviews at the mortem sites. A few people heard screams; I noted the times here." Ken handed him a notebook before checking his watch. "I gave Moira's drawings of the sites a cursory glance, but not a full review. No time. I've got to clean up before my appointment with Confid. If you need anything else, I'll be upstairs," he said on his way out the door.

Moira placed her own notes on the cluttered table of dailies. Her artist's eye didn't miss a trick. "You've been working on puzzles?"

"I'm allowed a moment between investigations."

"What are they?"

"Anagrams. Letters or words jumbled together, and using clues, you find a new word from it."

"A children's game?"

He hastily pushed the paper aside and reached for her drawing pad. "These scenes are, as I have come to expect, remarkable. Ramshackle buildings, but inside I see more evidence of children living there."

"Exactly. Each image is a place where a child was killed, but more than that, each scene represents a place where children lived. Toys, blankets, empty food crates. So the question now is, what happened to the ones who didn't die?"

"They ran."

"All of them? From every single site? All empty, never coming back? So where did they go?"

Patrick flipped through more of the drawings and swore at the very last. Two bicycles. He tapped the image. "They didn't go anywhere. They were taken. No one, kid or adult, would leave these behind. Not if they're on the move. This is good work, Moira. Amazing work."

"It means a lot to hear someone say it."

"No one has before?"

She shook her head. "Only as a curiosity."

"Then they're fools not to recognize it." And he knew a thing or two about low expectations. "You know, to many, I'm still just Clock's boy. I stay busy, mind, but it's always a matter of reaching out from beneath Matron's shadow. We both have things to prove, Moira."

Her tiny hand latched onto his and both eyebrows shot heavenward. "Then we shall prove it together."

"I would enjoy that." Hands still overlaid, he trapped her index finger. His breath caught at her smile. He coughed and tried to recover good sense as quickly as he could. "Any headaches?"

"I...yes. I drew a lot more than usual today."

The thought of her in pain left his gut riddled with guilt, and yet he needed her talent. He turned to get the small package wrapped with string and handed it over. "I had Catherine rustle up scrum bark for a tea to help with the pain. There's honey in there as well to temper the bitterness and lavender for a cold compress. If you need anything else, tell me and it's yours."

The furrow between her eyes lessened and those wonderful lips of hers lifted in a slight smile. "Honey? I don't need such extravagance. How on Earth did you get any?"

"I need you at your best, Gear. I can't have my brightest acquisition running a step behind."

He'd said it in jest, but demeaning his own gift looked to have demeaned her. Her smile dropped and her lips pressed into a straight line. "Thank you, Patrick."

She turned away, but his stupid, traitorous arm reached out for her. She gasped at his touch, huge eyes glistening at him over her shoulder. "I find it difficult to concentrate with the thought of you in pain running around my head. I prefer to avoid it."

And just like that her eyes lifted at the corners and he knew he'd jumped into dangerous waters. Damn.

She smiled.

He smiled back.

Double damn. "Dinner at five?"

"Dinner at five."

The warmth in the room left with her and he selfishly considered calling her back. He couldn't go on like this. The strength of character he'd been known for his entire life swirled around him as flotsam on the waves. What was it about her? Beauty? Intelligence? Spirit?

Yes.

Yes.

And yes.

Which placed him right back where he had been at the very beginning. Courtship. And putting her aside, that meant dealing with her parents. How, exactly, to tell a man that you've kept his daughter under your roof without benefit of escort, exposed her to corpses and put her in a first-hand fight against organized crime?

Not a good position to start from.

No, he had to solve the case first. Cases. All three of them. Once they proved her legitimate business here, matters of the private nature could take precedence.

Of course, that depended on the whether she felt the same. Her looks said so, or perhaps that was his imagination.

A ringing bell above stopped his sophomoric ruminations. Despite it being Ken's appointment, he adjusted his suit and got upstairs, eager for any distraction. With the absence of Catherine today, he had good reason and entered the receiving room pushing a tea service ahead of him.

Confid looked him over and went back to addressing Kennerick, whose grip on the armrest tightened until he worried the man's knuckles might pop out his skin.

Patrick poured his brother a cup and reached for another. When their cuckolded guest leaned forward, Patrick brought the cup to his own lips and took a seat on the opposite sofa.

The man gasped, head jerking from him to Kennerick. "Did you see what your boy just did?"

"There are no boys here. Patrick Clock, I present Baron Confid."

It was a hell of slight and one that might cost them the job. Even the lowest of London knew the rules of introduction, betters to lessers. The good baron's red face showed just how unused he was to that second-rung position. "Well I never. How dare you?"

Nothing Kennerick did ever went unplanned. While he waited to see just what that plan might be, Confid's chest puffed and he stomped out the door. Ken reached for the sugar. "I've decided to sleep with his wife for a while longer."

"Because?"

"Before coming down, I left the daily out and folded to an article about a missing child. When I walked in, the first thing he told me was that he wished more of the bastards would disappear."

"Is that a good enough reason to lose his business?" He wasn't cross, but when money was the matter, he did need to watch the bottom line.

"You came here as a baby, Patrick. Sometimes you forget that I didn't have the luxury. If it hadn't been for Matron's grace or had I chosen someone else's pocket to pinch, any one of those boys could have been me.

"I didn't mean anything by it." Kennerick's birth ranked top of the list of things not to be discussed. That he'd brought it up at all shouted what he thought of the baron's behavior. "Go on."

"Confid spilled that the family livery collar, his great-grandfather being a lord of somesuch place I've never heard of, was in need of repair. They sent off to the jeweler. When it was fixed, Confid sent two young house servants to pick it up, not detailing the contents therein."

"And it didn't make it back?"

"According to him, the boys stole it."

"But according to the boys?"

"They accused the older boys of waiting for them the second they crossed the street. After a private *interrogation*, Confid turned the servants over to the badges and paid a judge to ship 'em off to a workhouse."

"And after essentially enslaving them, still no collar?"

"Correct. The weight of a small child in gold, sapphire and emeralds, vanished quick as that."

"The obvious answer is the jeweler, but he'd value his business too much to have the goods disappear. Someone who knew the jeweler, then?"

Kennerick shrugged and propped his feet on the small coral table. "Someone who knew Confid. The man's a braggart, and this was one of the most expensive jewelry houses in London's tunnels. He'd have told anyone who would listen and anyone who shouldn't be listening."

"Staff?"

"Yes. Or a cash-poor lord. Who knows? I'll keep an ear out, and should the thing surface, I'll collect it, return it to Confid and still receive a handsome fee," he said with a wave in the air. "This will all be water under the bridge."

"And the wife?"

"I'll be done with her long before then."

Chapter VII

Patrick knew an angry woman when he saw one.

Moira stomped down the stairs to breakfast the next morning with a definite chill in her step. Things didn't improve from there. She stabbed at her oysters and seaweed, the fork screeching across the plate between the eye rolling and clicked tongue.

"Is there something wrong?"

Before she could answer, Kennerick excused himself and shut the door behind him. Bloody coward.

"Yes."

"Care to share?"

The fork-that-screeched quickly morphed into the fork-that-pointed. "It was my understanding that yesterday's appointment was meant to be between Doctor Kennerick and his potential client. Is that not what was said?"

"Fine. And?"

"And? AND? Why is that I heard no fewer than three voices?"

"I sat in."

"I surmised that, Mr. Clock."

"Back to mister already? It's not even noon."

"This is nothing to laugh about. Do you value my assistance?"

"Of course, I—"

"Then why wasn't I invited?"

"You were meant to be asleep."

"So my exclusion was planned by you."

"*You* said you had a headache. Not me. This was no slight, Moira. You're good and I want you around. If I didn't, you wouldn't be here. For the record, with you under *my* roof, your reputation isn't the only one on the line, thank you very much. Next time you decide to get your knickers in twist, find out if it's warranted. Anything else? Maybe you're mad because the water's blue?"

"I...well...no. Are you being honest? Never mind, you're an easy read. Am I meant to apologize now?"

"If it's not too distasteful."

"It does burn the throat a little."

He snorted and went back to his food, now gone tasteless. How could she think so little of him? His eyes kept wandering over to her across the short, but not short enough, table. "I value you, Moira. I promise you that against all I have. How's this? Kennerick will continue to press the ladies about town, but for our cases, we're at bit of a standstill. I've scoured the dailies until my eyes crossed in an effort to confirm your prior research. The next clue will have to come to us."

"We do nothing until something happens?"

"No. We go out."

"Out?"

"We go and see what there is to see. Talk to people. Together. You haven't had much of a chance to see London, have you?"

"I've been busy trying to solve crimes."

"If I may give some advice?"

"Please."

"Live," he said. And meant every letter of it. "I've been at this long enough to know that you have to fight for your humanity every so often. You still have yours, Moira."

"And you don't? What makes you so sure?"

"You reminded me that we're searching for children, not figures on a block. Kept me grounded. Allow me to return the favor. While investigating, this life is our everything. We work it. We come home to it. We wake up to it. We must not, however, be consumed by it. I won't let it happen to you."

"Let?"

"Let. Note the finality in my tone."

"I see."

He watched her go to war with herself, fingers tapping against the table's edge. But he knew the exact moment he'd won.

Kind of.

"One condition," she said. "I have a very handsome bicycle, one I'm sure I paid handsomely for."

"I've heard."

"I'm sure. Shall we take a ride to the Central Library? You're right, I've cross-checked dailies from home to here. It wouldn't hurt to see if there are similar goings about in the tunnels of Edinburgh or Dublin."

"The Wild Waters? If anyone's stealing boys from either of those places, we'd have heard the ruckus. "

"I still think it's worth a check. Even going back just three months."

"Then we'll lunch al fresco. Those boys' clothes should do just fine. We'll get you more in town."

Something flittered across her face, but before he could sort it, her smile beamed bright again. "Can do."

"And after that, maybe a quick trip to Newgate. I need to find out everything I can about this King Hellion."

"This sounds a bit like work, Patrick."

"We'll have to ensure it doesn't stay that way the whole day."

"As your erstwhile employee, I'll do my best."

While she went upstairs to change, and hell, he tried not to imagine it, he went through the stack of correspondence Catherine had left for him by the door. Bills. More bills. Requests for private meetings and...

Hmm...

A single kelp-laced envelope with nothing other than his name. That in and of itself wasn't unusual, but the script had him grasping for the wall in a feeble attempt to stay upright.

His name, strong as the moon itself, was written in Matron Clock's hand. "Grandma?"

There was no mistaking the perfect block and heavy lines of her handwriting, even though it waved a little through the tears that he tried to blink away.

He wanted to rip in two yet and yet was terrified.

Terrified it wasn't her.

Terrified it was.

Terrified to ruin anything she'd touched.

The paper rustled in his shaking and now sweaty hands. He brushed them against his pants, over and over again, desperate not to spread the ink:

She's perfect. Choose her. Fulfill the will.

"What?"

He flipped the note over, wiping tears now impossible to restrain on his shoulder. A single sheet of paper had reduced him to a crying child. "Damn you Kennerick."

It had to be him. He'd hired a forger and...and...

He took the stairs to Kennerick's room two at a time, not bothering to knock on his way inside.

The bastard lowered the book in his hand and had the fucking gall to raise an eyebrow. "The devil's wrong with you?"

"Too damned far, Ken!"

"Whatever it is you think I did, I didn't."

"Whale shit. Look!" He waved the letter as he approached, shoving it into his brother's face. "You do this again and I swear I'll kill you myself."

"Grandma."

That's it. One single word and Kennerick Dario Clock, one of the hardest men he knew, crashed to the floor. It couldn't be this broken, shaking man tracing the edges of the note with trembling fingers.

"You didn't do it."

Ken's head snapped up, teeth bared to a shark's edge. "That whore. I'll kill her."

"Ken!" He pulled him back from the door, forcing him against the bed. He had height and weight over Kennerick, but none of that had mattered before and certainly not today. It took every ounce of strength he had to hold him down.

"It was that fucking Moira—"

"Watch it!"

"Then who?"

"Think, Ken! Think! She didn't know. No one knows but you me and the solicitor."

Kennerick wrenched away, face redder than any coral in the waters. "I'll kill whoever did this."

"What if…"

"What? Grandma wrote it from the grave? Even she's not that good," he said with a chuckle completely devoid of humor. Kennerick punched the bedpost, even as he leaned against it. "I meant what I said, Patrick. I'll find the person who did this. Leave it to me."

"Don't touch her."

Ken didn't bother to look up. "You can't know her well enough to discount her. Maybe you're the one who needs to start thinking."

"I know enough. And I'm logical enough—"

"Not on this."

"She couldn't have known. You want to know where to look? Follow the solicitor. He gets his cut upon execution of the will. He must have seen us. I bet everything on it. When you get him to confess, and you will, save a piece of him for me."

"Promise me one thing before you go running back to your precious Moira."

"Ken—"

"Promise me that whatever I find, you'll support my decision to handle it the way I see fit. That shouldn't be a problem, seeing as how our lady investigator is as innocent as freshly fallen rain."

"If that's your way of testing my faith in her, then fine. I promise. You have free rein over the culprit as long as—"

"No conditions, Patrick."

Either he trusted Moira or he didn't. "Whoever is playing this sick game...agreed...no conditions. Don't come to me until it's solved."

"Fine."

He left Ken by window and walked into the hall, cracking his neck and willing his nerves to calm down. He was angry, yes, but the seed planted in their earlier conversation had been given new life with this note. The bastard who'd sent the letter, whoever he was, clarified a few points.

Firstly, that someone knew a woman, not a relation or servant, was in the house. That cut the most. The last thing he wanted to do was destroy her reputation, and yet it'd been the primary accomplishment. Hell, at this point, marriage was the most honorable thing he could do to her.

Secondly, the writer knew the contents of the will itself.

Had the solicitor been watching and waiting for any woman to come into their lives? Or was their ruse so transparent that anyone with eyes could have gone running their mouths to him?

There was no other explanation, as every short word of the note had been true. Especially the first part.

Kelp to kelp, she much preferred this Patrick to the any other. He smiled easily this morning, and without Kennerick's ruinous mood, breakfast left her refreshed and eager for the day. She still didn't have a cycling dress, but she didn't want Patrick to see her in trousers, either.

Despite her vehement protestations of wanting to work and the seriousness of what they had before them, she couldn't stifle the vain little part of her desperate to look pretty today. That meant quick work. A few darts with a needle here and there had her skirts hitched at the right points to avoid a nasty chain tangle. All for him.

He'd been kind. Caring. And most importantly, willing to listen. How different would life have been if the other men in her life had done the same?

The answer wasn't good. It was only because of her father and brother's foolishness that she'd come here. The greater question was of how different her life would have been if she and Patrick had gotten to know each other better back then.

Would they have married? Would that have bloomed into a proper partnership of mind and even heart?

Hair, yesterday pushed into a cap, was now brushed into submission. She braided it into six loose plaits, then wrapped them about her head and bobby pinned the ends to mimic a gentle wave. One bright blue ribbon, woven through the braids, gave her a hint of color. Bit by bit, she returned – the old her – the happy woman from Brighton.

Well, not exactly.

The woman she saw in the mirror was about to go walking with a man she wasn't promised to. It ought to have scandalized her, but she was a new woman of a new age. She dared him to send her back upstairs.

She noticed Patrick's feet first. One tapped as he waited for her at the bottom of the stair. It smacked of irritability. Then his eyes met hers and his slow, slack-jawed smile grew to ridiculous proportions. A self-congratulatory pat on the back might not be in order, but she knew she'd never forget his face. "I'm not late, am I?"

"No! Yes, not by much. So, no. You look...different."

"Is that bad?

"I didn't say that. It's just..."

"Since we've made our acquaintance, I've worn traveling clothes, household duds and slunk about town as an eager lad in the name of investigation. You won't begrudge this one day to be a proper lady, will you?"

To her annoyance, he got his faculties under control. "I should."

"You won't."

"We don't need to flaunt this."

"No one's watching."

"It's London. Everyone's watching, but there's no talking you out it, I'm sure. And let the record show, you've been more than proper. I can't say the same for Kennerick and myself."

She reached the bottom of the stair and waited for him to open the door before responding. "Kennerick is Kennerick. You're you."

"And you're learning to adjust to me? I must say, I'm at sixes and sevens with you. Most times I don't know whether to throttle you or..." His voice trailed off while he kneeled to release their bicycles from the catch.

She could do it. Now was the time. There was just enough shrubbery that if she knelt too, she might manage a kiss.

It was a wild thought.

A crazy fish swimming about in her head. It darted from one memory to the other – of them walking, talking, investigating and laughing.

"Or kiss me," she accidently-purposely said.

His hands froze, but his face turned upward, catching her smile. "Something like that."

"I'd let you."

"Moira, don't." He rose to his feet, bicycles clinking to the ground. "You deserve better than some quick muckabout."

"Awful high and mighty to think you'd get *that*. I offered a kiss. You should be slapped for that." Not that she was quite sure what *that* was, but she had enough of an idea to know he hadn't earned it. She was still her father's daughter. Despite coming way out here and leaving home...despite working in a field that would horrify her mother, she was their daughter. What she had to give to a man would be done at her place and time of choosing. Not even Patrick's lip-biting smile could change that.

But what was the harm in a little kiss?

He looked down at her, arms crossed, and shook his head. "Sixes and sevens. If I kiss you, little Moira, it might lead us down a dangerous path."

"More dangerous than the purpose of our travels today?"

"By leaps and bounds. You're too amazing a woman—"

"If you don't want to, I'm of no mind to make you."

"Want?"

And that was the last thing he said before his lips smashed against hers. Kisses were strange things. So very different with the slightest change of variables. Men had tried this before. She'd asked before, but those had been hesitant dry things.

Patrick's lips were like spiced tea, sweet and savory at once and filling her with warmth. Every part of him blazed heat. His hands splayed around her waist were like coils of a furnace. She'd gotten so hot that she wondered if the tunnel's heating mechanism had gone awry.

But no, this was all Patrick. Correction, she and Patrick, still the most amazing of cohorts. They were as good together as their lips were.

And improving...

His mouth opened and she mimicked the action when his tongue brushed at her lower lip. She ought to stop this. They were still standing, and at the right angle, someone might spot them.

But she didn't want to. Ever. She was happy here, in his arms and on his lips. And gracious, happiness was so hard to come by in this world. So, yes, from a purely logical standpoint, this was very, very good.

He cleared his throat and her face heated with embarrassment. Had he been trying to pull back all this time?

No.

Because the throat cleared again and Patrick's lips were still there.

Or had been.

They whirled around to spot a glowering Kennerick trotting down the steps. "Don't mind me, just out for my meatpie. I do hate to interrupt, but if I could just get my bicycle, I'll on my way. No need to stop on my account. Carry on."

Yes, they had been. Hesitant eyes drifted up to Patrick, who at once looked embarrassed and angry and yet with the same silly grin she felt on her own face. He grimaced at Kennerick, then turned to her and smiled. He repeated this bit of silent theater twice more, until Kennerick pedaled away, looking back and shaking his head.

When they were alone again, she found it quite impossible to think of what to say. Her would-be paramour, nee employer, didn't speak either. Instead, he handed over her bicycle, hopped on his own, and in silence they took to the streets.

It was the best and most filled silence she'd ever known. One punctuated by random chuckles and accented with sly looks at intersections. It was the kind of easy quiet of camaraderie and genuine affection that left no room for shame or regret, but peace and perhaps the promise of future kisses.

A promise she'd make sure to keep.

Too soon they came upon the police station, but he pedaled past it for several streets, not stopping until they reached the postal office. He had the same easy look about him when they stopped, save his eyes. They'd narrowed in easy-to-read determination.

"Do you think there's something here?"

"I think you should write to your parents."

"Patrick—"

"I won't have your father thinking I'm taking advantage of you, Moira."

"He doesn't even know I'm here."

"All the more reason to write."

All the more reason not.

"But he'll show up. I know he will."

"Do you care for me?"

"I...well...you know the answer that."

"I'd like to hear it."

"You respect me. Not just me, but my work. You treat me as a man and –"

"I don't kiss men, Moira Gear."

"Stop it. You know what I'm trying to say. I don't wish to go back when this investigation is over."

"So you wish to stay on as an employee?" His eyes hadn't left hers, needling right into her soul.

"I wish...to stay. I think. Oh, I was ruined from the moment I left home alone. What does it matter now?"

"Everything. If you're my staff, that's one thing and can be contained. Perhaps." He stepped closer and bent until their faces were inches apart and his breath tickled her face. "But if I mean to court you, and I do, we've gone too far outside the bounds of respectability already. How can we decide what happens next if there's no proper courtship to get to know one another?"

"This is *our* proper courtship. Flowers and cards won't do for me."

"You deserve those things."

"I deserve what I want. Sketches. More graphite for my pencils. The odd murder scene or two."

With his snort, the tension that swirled around them dissipated to slush. Most of it. "I doubt your father will see it that way."

She took out a pad and pencil and spoke aloud as she wrote. "Dear Father and Mother, I'm well and happy. I am responsible for solving no less than two crimes, though my name has been redacted for obvious reasons."

"Solved?"

"Well, we will have by the time this reaches them." She started again. "I'm earning enough for room and board at a respectable establishment."

Another snort.

"With a proprietor who cares more for propriety than I care to mention."

If the man snorted again, she'd *thwap* him.

"In summation, I am happily accomplishing what I set out to and so much more. Please hold on to that, and not your cross feelings. Warmly and lovingly, Moira."

"There's a lady renting rooms—"

"Don't you start. I'm ruined already."

"Stop staying that. You're not. We can still fix it."

"Exactly. I know that and you know that. Who else matters?"

"What kind of marriage...not that...I mean..."

She folded the note and took out a tuppence for an envelope. "You have a terrible habit of getting ahead of yourself. Be a dear and run this in for me?"

Marriage.

The word hung between them like a leaden weight, and the confirmation of that was on his sagging shoulders as he entered the postal office.

Well, he'd said it, not her. They hadn't known each other long enough to begin to address it...yet people had been forced to marry for far less than what they'd done.

Not that it was *off* the table either. After all, it would take a man like Patrick to handle her. What were the chances she'd find someone like him again?

Infinite zero.

The longer she thought about it, the more sense he made. That house needed a woman in it and she needed a home. They were attracted to one another, no denying that. They worked well together too. And this career! From her earliest years, she'd wanted to be an investigator and stand as a bulwark against crime like her brother. And yet, those who loved her most dearly would keep her from it.

Not Patrick.

He didn't love her and yet he still gave her more consideration than they ever did.

But he might love her one day.

Or not.

Best to ask.

He came down the stairs with a look on his face that meant business. She didn't fail to notice the note still in his hand. "Listen, Moira—"

"Would you like to marry me?"

"What?"

"I've been thinking—"

"I see that."

"We get on well together and you find me attractive, don't you?"

"None of this is proper."

"Well, why not? Stop shaking your head and look at me. Every marriage these days is a business arrangement. We should look at ours the same way."

"You make it sound a fait accompli."

"It is. Let's be honest, Patrick. No one else would have me."

"Any man with good sense would."

"And there's the rub. Sensible men are few and tragically far between. Then there's you who accepts me for who I am. I know you're not getting a fair deal out of the bargain, but you'll never find a woman who understands your life as well as I do. Consider it a business merger, no different than any other."

"A tad different. A tad. And what do I do when you're walking home years from now and find the man you truly are meant to love?"

"Who says it can't be you? No one marries for love outside of penny theatricals. Marriages are all contracts and acquisitions."

Patrick's face tightened, and she turned away whilst her heart beat a steady drum of humiliation. Stars, she'd ruined everything. She'd taken one word out of his mouth and run with it. Now he couldn't stand to look at her, and her career slipped through her fingers. Never mind the man. Perhaps it was a good thing that he hadn't posted the letter.

"I should be a better gentleman than this."

"I understand. No matter. It's...I'll go and get my things. I won't abandon the case, though. I can't. I'll work alone."

"I want a marriage, not a transaction."

"I heard you the first time."

"With you, Moira. I fancied you from the first time I saw you, but I deserve better than an agreement. So do you. You should receive gifts—"

"Life a knife?"

"Flowers."

"You'll buy me some on the way home."

"What if we don't take to one another?"

"Then we have the business to fall back on. 'The Clocks of London.' See? I won't even ask you to change the name of the business."

"Do you mean to bully me into marriage?"

"I do, Patrick."

"That was good."

"Thank you."

"But still not enough."

Her lips parted in aborted speech and she tried turning away. His finger on her chin stopped her. "You see me as a means to an end. I see you as...as a prize to claim. A woman of beauty and mind? I'll take that bet and we'll grow magnificent out of it. New letter home. You write, I dictate."

Stomach fluttering, she whipped out her pad, leaned against the post office railing and started penning this new letter. Some of the lines were a bit wobbly and a few letters had shaky starts and some of the lines were too heavy, a visual recording of the surprise she felt at his words. Still, by the end of it, she had to admit it just might be the finest of letters anyone could have received. She gave it a once over, folded it and took it up the gray steps herself.

Chapter VIII

Had he just agreed to marriage?

He deserved to be beaten. He deserved to be taken to task and have every man in her family come down and throttle him. Hell, might happen anyway.

And he'd never felt better.

He'd confessed to the crime of seduction, though she'd been the one to seduce him as far as he could tell. Most of the letter, however, was true and to the point. They'd met while investigating a case. She confirmed that she was staying at a boarding house and he, good man that he was, was merely writing a letter to verify all she'd said was true. Finally, he noted he had placed her in a home of good repute with a lady of peerage, as of way of settling her into the city and serving as chaperone.

Because yes, he'd stated his intentions.

Courtships could last months, and that might buy him time depending on the man her father was. If Lord Gear was the sort who loved his daughter more than his pride, he'd come down straight away. To the converse, if the man valued pride above family, to hell with him, but he had to make things right as best he could for Moira's sake.

Matron's will flickered on the dull lights in his brain. All this time he'd had it wrong. Her will hadn't been a challenge or a curse. It'd been Matron's final blessing. He'd tell Moira, get it over with and hope she understood.

"Patrick?"

"Just thinking of my grandmother. She left a..."

Moira's bright eyes and upturned mouth snatched the words from his throat. She looked so happy, excited and...damn. It'd do

Moira no good to have her thinking he'd used her only to get the money from the will.

"She left what, Patrick?"

"She left a hole in our hearts. I wish you could have met her."

"Me too." She nodded and looked to the east. "So tell me about this woman you told my Papa I'm living with," she said, handlebars in hand.

They biked at an urchin's pace toward their next stop, a prostitute's home, as casually as going to the theatre. He wasn't quite sure how to break the news. "She's an old friend."

"Sounds scandalous."

"Quite. She used to work in a brothel. Now she owns one."

"No! May I ask how you came to meet this soiled dove?"

"Kennerick's older sister." He grabbed her handlebars to keep her on two wheels. "Try not to be too shocked. She raised him as best she could before Grandmother took him in. Go on, ask. Mind the cart ahead of you."

She swerved around the mollusk vendor and they reconnected on the other side. "It's none of my business."

"No?"

"Well—"

"No, we haven't. She's a sister of sorts. Nothing more. You'll like Anastasia." He watched Moira as much as the road. Her assessment of the woman would be a testimony to herself. Would she hold it against her? Him?

To her great credit, Moira didn't look upset or disgusted. More curious than anything, if he had to guess. Fair enough.

"Will I get a chance to meet her?"

"If you like. Whatever you think of her, she did what she had to do to put food in Ken's mouth. She mothered him more than the woman that birthed them."

"What happened to her?"

"Who knows? She walked away from them their whole lives. Each time she'd leave them alone for longer spells until one day, she didn't come back at all. It's a case Ken's never had an interest in solving. I know he's not the warmest man, but don't judge him too harshly. He's had a rough go of it."

"I see."

But he could tell by her face that she didn't. Not quite. "Anything else?"

"Not on your end. The rest will have to be settled between Kennerick and myself directly. As for his sister, my father will investigate your story. Hers too."

"I expect so. Don't worry. We set up a history and lineage for Anastasia years ago. She ensures that her daily business is done by middlemen, that is, middlewomen. Her hands are pure on every legal front. Turn here. There's a cut-through at the station."

"We have a very strange family, you and I."

"I like the sound of that. We."

"Me too. Look at us, mooring about like children. I'm not marrying you for your good looks, Clock. Or your kisses or your family. Only your cases." She hopped off her bicycle at the police station. "After you."

"Is this my new life? To be pushed around? I won't stand for it."

"You will."

He would. Damn them both for it.

And so it was that he walked into the police station a nearly married man to his ex-schoolmate's sister.

Fine.

Better than fine.

And it provided a benefit, beyond the obvious. While they'd been lucky in avoiding neighbors, they'd need an excuse to be seen about together. As his affianced, however, society would expect them to spend their days in each other's gaze, and for a man like himself, that meant days at the station.

"What a wonder. You're getting married, Clock? Well, congratulations!" Chief Detective Policeman Bane shook his hand until his arm near fell out of the socket. "But you bring her here, lad?"

"I truly don't mind," Moira said with a flick of her fan. "He's told me about his work and the wonderful job you do here. To say that he holds you in high esteem is to grossly understate the claim. I am in awe of what you accomplish and, oh, I fair begged him to bring me."

Bane's peppery mustache twitched. An unexpected blush crept from beneath it. "I do try my best. Protecting the tunnels and hubs of London is what I live for."

"That's what Patrick told me. It took much begging, but he allowed me to sit in on an investigation. Or will, that is, if it's all right with you." Her voice went higher the longer she talked, until it bore an almost childlike innocence. That, combined with the batted eyes and strangely placed trills of laughter, had Bane eating from her cupped and perfumed palms.

Clock had never seen a better performance. Good gracious, the legends of the stage could learn a thing from Moira...and Bane. With a rapt and captive audience, the detective policeman made a grand show of charts and maps, hands flailing in every direction. "I blame it all on them Hellion boys."

"All of what?"

"He didn't tell you, ma'am? No, I imagine not. Far too much for delicate ears."

"Oh, please. Patrick, let him tell me."

He fought the urge to roll his eyes. At his nod, Bane leaned over the desk, beady eyes glistening. "Brazen thievery in some of the most upstanding of places."

"My word. Do you think it has anything to do with those missing children?"

"I'd hardly call them children, Miss. Scoundrels from the birth, I'd say. Blood will tell. No, I don't think they're missing. Gone underground perhaps or moved to another city with pilfered goods. You know how boys are."

"All boys?" she asked.

"Quite. All males, which bolsters the point, doesn't it? I reckon boys join up with Hellion, earn a bit of scratch, then head off on their own. Who knows? Every boy that age wants to take his chance on land. Maybe they went to one those above-water countries. But don't you worry your pretty little head about it. I'll find this Hellion and set London to rights."

"I'm sure that you will. Oh, dear, I fear all this talk of criminality has my head in an awful tizzy. I feel quite faint. Just the thought of them roaming about. Oh, dear!"

By heavenly grace did he manage to catch her before she tumbled to the floor. At her supremely smooth call for an exit, Patrick jumped to his feet and fanned her face. "I need to get her to Kennerick, Bane. You'll excuse us?"

"Of course. I didn't mean to overexert the girl."

"She's from Brighton."

"Say no more. Poor lass. These loud and bustling tunnels are too much for small-water folk. You'll have a time with her."

"Too right." The *poor lass's* eyes fluttered and he shifted to prevent Bane seeing Moira's lips curl in a barely suppressed smile. She leaned heavily on him, back heaving, leaving other officers to stop what they were doing to look on woefully.

The heaving was the laughter threatening to bubble to the surface. He got them out of there and on their bicycles just in time. Her giggling led the way as they pedaled down lanes and cross streets like children on the lam from school. At the park, they stopped for a breather, sitting a respectable distance apart. Too far.

The space was mostly sand and gravel – grass parks being only available in the most exclusive of tunnels – but she looked natural here, drawing small circles with the toe of her boot.

Moira pulled a kerchief from her sleeve and dabbed at her temple. "I've never seen such behavior. This is the man who keeps London safe?"

"No. That would be the other policemen in the building. Bane is simply the man in charge. You, on the other hand, were magnificent. Fancy work back there."

She gave a mock bow and wave. "Thank you, thank you. As much as I detest men who think that way, I'm not averse to using their small-mindedness to our advantage."

"Our?"

"I...I mean..."

"That the small matter of our impending nuptials should be so quickly glossed?"

"I was concerned with much bigger issues, Patrick. For instance, our cases. Our friendship. I put them far above a piece of paper that society requires for us to maintain both."

There she was again, successfully soothing an impossible situation. And him. He'd found the woman of his dreams in the worst of circumstances but was too much of a bastard to let her go. But if she saw this as a business exchange, what was the harm in it? She'd love him soon enough. Right? "You can leave at any time."

"Do you want me to?"

"No."

"I didn't spare a thought about a bicycle when I came to London."

"So?"

She shrugged. "Now I have one."

"This is a little bigger than that. I didn't mean for it to happen this way."

"Thus implying you meant for it to happen in some way?"

He cleared his throat and shook his head, choosing his words carefully. "Every man wants a wife."

"So any woman would do."

Was that a question? He didn't know, but before he could answer, Moira turned away and toed a clod of gravel. "And now you have one."

Chapter IX

She spent the next week in a state of grinning shock. With all leads temporarily tapped out, she and Patrick passed each day getting to know one another. They lunched. They took in plays and recitals. They biked around the city, blending in with ease among the happiest of tourists.

He was ever the gentleman...even with the open invitation for kisses. Twice she'd leaned in and twice he'd pulled back. At least one of them still had a bit of modesty. Or had he lost interest already?

No.

Impossible. He smiled more and more each day. He really was just a good man. And now her good man wanting to save her reputation.

This won.

On the great long list of impossible and improbable things she'd done, this won top ribbon. Though their romance, if one could call it that, hadn't involved love at first sight, they had respect, a rare thing in any betrothal.

Respect and the opportunity to continue this wild pursuit of her dreams. And love could come. Someday.

Would come.

And at this rate, sooner than later.

Because she liked him. Really liked him. And they held each other in high esteem, and to be very honest, that meant so much more. She'd done everything else on her own terms. Why not marriage?

Kennerick sat at the top of the stairs, one hand resting on his chin. "You're marrying him?"

"Have you been waiting for me to come out of my room?"

"Yes. Well?"

"To answer your question, yes. Probably."

"Probably?"

"I reserve the right to change my mind."

"But you proposed."

"Yes."

"Not him?"

"No. Well, it was rather mutual."

Kennerick swore and clapped his hands. "Oh, he's good."

"Excuse me?"

"And on the condition that you can *un*propose?"

"Correct."

"Why wasn't I told about this earlier?"

"Well, I'm not marrying you, am I?" The doctor rocked back, lips mouthing words, though nothing escaped. "Have I finally managed to render you speechless?"

"Close. Very close. Let's move on to more important matters than you."

Just who did he think he was? Her fingers itched to slap that smug look off his face, but the fact that this man would be her brother someday stayed her hand. "More important?"

"I'm having sod all success with the medical records on my end. I'm diving a little deeper, and you need to attend an autopsy."

"Are you mad?"

"The body's in the attic."

"You are mad."

"I'm desperate and time is short. They found another child today. I paid my arse to get the examiner's wagon to drop him off, but they will be back in less than an hour. That leaves me little time to review the body, open him and—"

"You can't ask me to do this."

"I'm not asking and you have to do it right now. Every moment we waste is lost information. One does not simply die, Moira. It is a long process that takes hours. Each second we argue deteriorates more evidence. We have to capture what we can right now and I need your eye for that. Will you walk or do I need to carry you?"

She could fight him. Scream. Hit. She had every right to stand her ground. She'd thrown a long line of talk about equality, but this went too far.

Didn't it?

Her weakness shamed her. Faced with an opportunity to act upon achieving that hard-won parity, she faltered.

"Well?"

"You'll forgive me if I don't charge upstairs with a smile on my face."

"Typical." The man's chin jutted out and his eyes narrowed. "You really are only good for the money."

"What on Earth are you talking about?"

The delight with which the next words fell out of his mouth sickened her. The corner of his lips raised, beautiful and cruel. "He's locked out of his inheritance until he marries. My, my, he hasn't told you? Pity. Welcome to the real world. Are you going to cry now or help solve this case?"

He said more, but the words jumbled beneath the throbbing of her heart. Patrick had played her for a fool. It had to have been his plan from the second he's forced himself into her room.

Her throat collapsed on itself and her eyes burned. Kennerick's gaze followed her every move, though, and she wouldn't let him see her cry. None of them would. "All of that is immaterial. Take me to the subject."

"Fine."

Her feet moved quite on their own. Her mind scrambled in vain to put the ache in her chest aside for the matter at hand. She'd seen a child in death's embrace before but knew this time would be different. Felt it, cold wrapping so tightly about her soul that she wished for a shawl about her to warm the prickly bumps on her arms.

Patrick had told her never to enter Kennerick's workspace. Now she knew why. It was more a maze than an office. Towering bookshelves cast looming shadows, filled with tomes and strange artifacts that seemed to reach out and grab the air.

It had a strange color about it too. Rooms glowed yellow or blue, depending on the type of lighting used. Not here. In the midst of strange instruments with backlit and liquid-filled containers, each section of the room carried its own hue, drawn from the contents of the glasses.

Even calling them glasses was a stretch. They *looked* to be of the material but twisted and coiled in strange shapes. Some burned, as evidenced by bubbles and drops of mist. Others iced over. "What is this?"

"No time. The body."

What she saw around the corner turned her anxious marvel to despair. Too blue and far too small.

"Aged seven to nine," Kennerick said, in a voice devoid of any emotion.

"How can you be clinical about this?"

"Appears in good health at time of death. No visible signs of—"

Tears blurred her vision and she bit her lip to keep it from trembling. "I've never seen..."

"I presume the others were more fresh?"

"We are not discussing the quality of food, Doctor. Look at you, ready to cut him open! Do I have to continually remind everyone in this household that these are children?"

Kennerick slammed a handful of scalpels and scissors against the table. "Exactly. Children. These are the tools of my trade, Moira. On that table are yours. Pick up the graphite. Pick up the paper and do your job. I'll do mine and together we'll work to make sure this doesn't happen to another one. Do you think I enjoy this?"

"It's a desecration."

"It's a duty. Because no one else can be bothered. Either they don't care or they refuse to get their hands dirty." He stopped, looked at the boy and made an incision from his throat to his navel. "Well, I do and I will. This child died without a name, but he carries with him his story. We will glean as much as we can from it. His hands. His nails. His entrails. His lungs. His heart. Any one may hold the key. Now draw or pick up your pretty skirts and run back to Brighton."

Patrick read Kennerick's note. Twice. Their dear solicitor had taken a much-needed holiday days before the mysterious letter arrived. That as good sealed it in his eyes that he was the fool who'd written it.

Not that he disagreed with the content, but he wasn't one to be pissed on. The second the arse got back into town, Kennerick would be waiting with fists and a transfer of governorship of the will. He refused to let the bastard profit off Moira. That settled, he turned to their other matters and reviewed his case notes.

Almost immediately, the words merged and swirled together. Patrick twisted his back to one side until it cracked, then reversed the move, determined to force his slow-witted brain on the words. The dull ache intensified as the minutes progressed, slithering its way from his temple and down his neck. He'd been bent over his desk too long. His own hands rubbing the knots loose didn't do much good for his back.

Would Moira do this for him one day? Stroke his aching muscles? Bring him peace?

He'd move all the waters to do it for her.

She occupied more and more of his thoughts while his cases took less and less. No good. Playing the besotted fool wouldn't do for his manhood, and yet his *manhood* was very much in working order. Obnoxiously so.

He spent ridiculous moments plotting how the rest of his life would go. He liked that – plans and order. The introduction of that black pearl oyster upstairs ruined it in the most delicious ways. Everything about her, beginning with the moment they'd met, brought glorious disruption.

The accounts and figures before him did little to erase the image of her from his mind, but he tried concentrating once again. He'd have to be an executive director *and* a husband now. With her, the two were inextricably entwined. Being the man Moira needed cemented the necessity of success. She, Kennerick, Catherine, McCoy and all those faceless boys demanded it. He'd be damned if he let them down.

Patrick made a list of the places from the burglary markings on Bane's map. Some he knew well. Others required a little footwork. Had Moira been able to draw, he'd know everything down to the house number and the color of the drapes. This methodology reduced him to the old style of investigation Matron taught him. There was some comfort in that. He missed the old days. There was no doubt the grand dame would have loved Moira for a whole host of reasons, starting with the beauty of her mind.

Well, damn.

A vision that could never be, Matron and Moira laughing over a shared table cracked his heart in half with its impossibility. Her scream from upstairs shattered the rest.

He bolted from the room, leaving a trail of papers fluttering to the floor in his wake. Hand on the knife he kept in his pocket, he'd gut anyone touching her. Kennerick might get there first, and he willed the man to leave some of the intruder for himself.

"Moira? MOIRA!"

It went against his training. He should have gone up quiet, snuck in and attacked from the back, but fear addled his mind. He needed to hear something other than her panic, but there was nothing but more screams.

He kicked open her door but was met by blood-boiling cries louder than before. In the dim light, his eyes surveyed one side of the room to the other before landing on her, legs drawn up to her chest and stiletto in hand. "Patrick?"

"Where is he?"

"He who?"

"The intruder."

She sniffed and shook her head. "There's no one."

"It's all right, Moira. He won't hurt you. Just tell me where he is."

"Patrick? Are you well?"

"Me? You screamed bloody murder and now you have a knife in your hand."

"Because someone kicked in my door."

"I know. Who?"

"You."

She'd gone mad from fright. He hadn't thought that possible from her. This was his fault. All of it. He should have never put her in this danger. Voice soft, he approached the bed, eyes searching every dark corner before dropping to a knee. "I heard you screaming before that."

She leaned over the edge too, eyes wide. "What are you looking for under the bed?"

He'd cracked her. "Darling—"

"I had a dream. I screamed myself awake, I suppose."

A dream?

Relief eased the weight off his chest. Lungs agreeing to work again, he let out a whoosh of air and sat on the bed, waiting for good sense to return.

No.

Not a bed.

Her bed.

He jettisoned up, but Moira's tugging on his sleeve brought him back down again. "Stay."

"This is inappropriate."

"You kicked in my door."

"To save you."

A shaky smile played across her face. "It wasn't locked." The smile didn't quite reach her glistening eyes and new tears started to fall. "I know about the will, Patrick. You should have told me."

"Moira—"

"I'm fine and understand the nature of our agreement, but I didn't appreciate having it thrown in my face."

"Kennerick?"

"Who else? The point is—"

"The point is that I don't do anything I don't want to. Not for all the money in the world. Nothing changes, Moira. Every reason we discussed still holds. You must marry, I should marry and your lips are still soft. Your mind, still brilliant."

With her head bent, he couldn't make out whether his words had an effect. Had he said enough?

No.

"It's true what I said in the park, then. That any girl would do?"

"Not any girl, Moira. You."

As if completely giving up on everything, she leaned into his chest and cried for all she was worth. He apologized until his throat ran dry, but nothing he said calmed her down. "I'm missing something. Tell me."

"I fear it will never leave my mind. I took two baths but the scent won't go either."

"Moira, tell me and I'll fix it."

He seethed as she spoke of it, gathering the will to choke the life out of Kennerick with his bare hands. He'd gone too damned far this time.

"I'll never get it out my mind. I'll always hate this day."

"We'll need to give you new memories, then. It's not too late – there's still an hour left. May I kiss you?" It was the worst thing to ask, but he didn't regret it. Not after she nodded. Not after she lifted her head and his lips cushioned upon hers.

They were as soft as he'd remembered.

As sweet, too.

And worth savoring.

He tried to be a better man. Really, he did and even tried standing, but she latched onto his arm, holding him in place. Next time he'd fight a little harder, but not today.

Her hands wrapped about his neck, drawing him close. She was unpracticed. Her soft lips didn't part for him as a lover's would. But stars love her, she was a damned fast learner. His tongue darted out, teasing at the swell of her bottom lip. She smiled against his mouth, granting him that much more access. He took it, pushing her down against the mattress.

He had to leave. Should leave, but didn't have the strength.

"Please, Patrick. I think we should...umm...stop."

The wouldn'ts and couldn'ts burned to a crisp at her soft-spoken and breathless command. He froze still as a glacier, grounded himself and pulled back, nuzzling her chin with his nose as his final sign of retreat. "You're right. I should go."

"I don't want that, either."

"I need you to be very clear with what you mean by that."

When she lay back, he almost had to hold his foot to the floor to avoid falling down next to her. But she turned on her side and reached for his hand. "Will you sit with me until I fall asleep?"

Sit here on the bed and not get her inside it? She meant to kill him. Every inch of his anatomy stood poised and ready to march on to glory, but more than craving her body, he needed her trust.

Nothing other to do than drag a chair over, hoist his feet on the side table and hold her hand as she drifted off to sleep under his watchful eyes.

He'd deal with Kennerick tomorrow.

Chapter X

When she woke the next morning, the man who'd called her "darling" while she cried was still there. Patrick snored deep in his chest, a strange thing to hear. How he'd found sleep in such an uncomfortable position, she couldn't fathom a guess. Dare she risk rising? No, best not. It must have taken him ages to get comfortable in that chair. On the other hand, she couldn't just wait for him to wake up. He needed to be out of here before Kennerick or Catherine started walking about the house. "My chest hurts."

"Huh?" Patrick groaned and sat up, thumbing sleep from his eyes. "I'll get Kennerick."

"Hold off a tick. With my superior skills of deductive reasoning, I've narrowed the cause down to two things. Embarrassment or endearment."

He smiled mid-yawn. "A proper detective resolves things to a final cause."

His hand brushed back a bit of hair that'd come loose from her braid during the night. Intimate and innocent, but it left her wanting more of his touch. "Will you kiss me?"

The words escaped on their own, but there was no worry he'd refuse. Something flickered in his eyes one half breath before he peeled back the covers. This man, *her* man, grabbed her by the waist and hoisted her up to her knees and his mouth.

This kiss was a whole lot different than the one before. As if the whole weight of his being came down on her lips, their mouths crashed together, bonded as closely as the panels of the tunnels. Something flickered inside her too. A deep burning in the pit of her body. She wanted this.

Wanted him.

Wanted more.

And leaned in to take it. Patrick moaned against her and started to draw back. A hooked arm around his neck stopped that foolishness.

"You don't know what you're doing, Moira."

"I'm not a fool."

He pried her interlaced fingers apart. "And I'm not a saint."

"Neither am I."

The man actually moaned. He also did a lot of loud exhaling and untangling and backwards walking to the door. "You're dangerous," he said, and slipped out of the room.

Hands locked over her mouth, she collapsed against the pillows. She'd been wild and reckless and loved every moment of it. He'd come when she needed him, even without truly being asked. A gentleman would have knocked or sent for a woman to enter her bedchamber. Patrick, however, was a man and he'd handled it his way – broken doorjamb and all. His presence hadn't erased the horrors of yesterday, but he had been there to see her through the night, and that meant everything.

She'd fight hook and line to keep that.

And someone fought just as much outside her doors. She scrambled into loose trousers and a blouse as the shuffling, grunting sounds of brawling drifted away. Not that they'd died down, but the fighting was migrating elsewhere.

By the time she was decent enough to step into the hallway, Patrick had just ducked a swing by Kennerick, while landing one of his own. She ran, arms outstretched, desperate to break apart the two men. "Stop it! Stop this right now!"

The men pivoted at her words, fists still ready for action. As if nothing was the matter, Kennerick bowed. "Good morning. I was just explaining to Patrick here how much of a boon you were yesterday. We didn't quite have time to get to the crux of it, but now that you're here, I'll say it once to both of you. Chemicals were used in the boy before the murder – of the sort used before one goes surfaceside."

Patrick rubbed a bloody lip against his shoulder. "For land oxygenation? Why would someone want to take these boys above? Boat workers?"

Kennerick gingerly pinched the bridge of a bloody and swollen nose. "It gives a new direction. The pupils were exactly the same as in the other drawing. There's no question of it."

"I'm glad it's settled, but I won't be able to help you again. Not like that, anyway."

Kennerick massaged his jaw and tongued his split lip. "Agreed. Off for my morning meatpie." Without a backward glance, he waved a hand above his head and started down the steps.

Patrick shrugged, swore, shoved his hands in his pockets and went down the hall to his own bedroom. He stopped halfway. "Breakfast at eight?"

"Breakfast at eight." And she said it knowing that Patrick considered the issue solved. She'd never be called upstairs to assist again.

Unless she wanted to. Maybe she would, but it would her choice and hers alone. That's what he'd given her – it's what he'd always given her. Choice. Though she hadn't been so generous. She'd forced herself into his home, his career and his life.

Yet men like Patrick weren't easily moved.

Her mind went back to the shy boy she'd met so long ago and compared him to the man he'd grown into.

No. Patrick hadn't been forced.

Or cajoled.

Or anything other than patient.

She still wasted precious seconds leaning against the silver and pearl door, grinning like a madwoman. After a cleanup in the basin, she opted for more subdued clothes today: blue flouncy trousers and a pressed blouse. Catherine had already set the table and prepared the morning soup by the time she made it down. They wouldn't be disturbed. The woman's broom swished across the floor in the next room, leaving her and Patrick alone.

"Business or pleasure?" he asked. "Juice?"

"Please and pleasure."

"You're looking lovely today. I remember those pants from school. They've never looked so good. Thought we might go on a walk, an actual walk with no other expectations. No crimes to solve, no clues to investigate. A day for us."

"And had I chosen business?"

He got up to fill her cup, bringing with him a strong scent of cologne. Had he always worn it, or was it stronger than usual for her sake?

"I'd planned around that," he said once he got back to his seat. "I was going to make up some excuse about the mind needing rest to enhance performance."

"According to some, it's true."

"Well there you are. With you, Moira, business is pleasure."

"But there's something else. I can see it in your eyes."

"You know me so well already?" He shoved a turtle egg in his mouth and took a sudden interest in his turtle soup. "Fine. I sent a note to Kennerick's sister this morning."

"Letting her know her part in the story?"

He looked up. Barely. "Expanding it. I'd like for you to move in with her."

"At the brothel?"

"She keeps a separate house."

"And that's somehow less suspicious than staying here?"

His fork clanked against the plate. "Enormously so."

"You're wrong. I'm not leaving. Can you pass the salt, please?"

"With pleasure and you are."

She grabbed the bar of salt and shaved a touch of it across her eggs. "Thank you. I'm not. I never figured you to be concerned about what others think."

"It's about doing what's right, Moira."

"What changed between yesterday and today?"

"Umm, yesterday."

"Patrick—"

"Putting aside your family, you still have to live in this neighborhood once this is over, or started, as the case may be. I won't have you talked about."

"I don't care. If I was so worried about others, I wouldn't be here in the first place."

"Then think about the children. Our children. Not that...well..."

"Are you worried that people will say something to these imaginary children of ours, or more worried that they will come too early?"

"Moira Gear!"

"I trust you, Patrick."

"I'm not the problem."

Well, she couldn't *not* laugh. "You're scared of me."

"No. Yes. Terrified."

"We will be married one day..."

"What the hell are you saying?"

She couldn't price the look on his face. She knew desire. She'd seen it directed her way plenty of times. Patrick's face had the same look, a mixture of sharpness and weakness. He wanted her, and a devilish part inside wanted to know what he'd do when he got her.

Michael and his friends whispered about lovemaking when they thought no one else was around to hear it. The thought of her brother doing those things to someone made her positively ill. The thought of Patrick doing it to her turned her in quite the opposite direction. "Ours is a story of appreciation. I appreciate how much you've trusted me to manage myself and my affairs. I appreciate that you appreciate my sound mind and logic. You're a clever man, but I'll appreciate you even more once you realize that I will continue my life according to my own mind. I trust that mind. It led me here."

"I thought it was me dragging you out of a slum that did it?"

"If that's what you need to believe."

His rumbling laughter didn't change anything. He'd still sent the letter and she still had no intention of going. Patrick dabbed at the corner of his watering eyes with his napkin, mumbled something akin to dragging them both into madness and leaned over to drop a kiss on her cheek.

Just one.

She wouldn't mind another, but if the big, scary, tough investigator was skittish, she didn't need to give him any room for panic. "There. No letter is necessary. I didn't attack you. You didn't attack me. I'll continue dressing as a boy when we leave the house. The costume will allow me to move freely—"

"You won't trick anyone."

"I already have. I'm good at it. You know me, but most won't spare a passing glance."

"And when I need a woman at my side?"

"We'll have an escort in Kennerick's sister."

He plucked an envelope from an inner pocket of his waistcoat and ripped it in two with flair and ceremony. "I suppose—"

"I should have known you hadn't sent the letter yet."

"I meant to on our walk."

"No you didn't."

"I did."

"I'm not calling you a liar. The inner you intended for me to stop you."

"No, I—"

"Trust me. I'm an investigator."

What had she done to him?

He pushed his bicycle a few steps ahead of her and hated himself for letting it come to this. Desperately he wanted to reach back, take her arm in his and walk as a proper couple should. Thus the rub. To have that privilege, he'd have to give something up. Her in his house for starters.

They stopped at Anastasia's pink and white townhome, entering with a nod to the girl who answered the yellow-trimmed door. He never bothered to learn their names. Anastasia's house was a training ground of sorts – a place where some of her aging working girls learned the niceties of society before being sent out as respectable nannies and housemaids. The woman did a wobbly bob before seeking out her mistress.

Moira ran her hand along the back of a plush, purple chair in the drawing room. "It's not what I imagined."

"What? Expecting dancing girls on my stairs?" asked a crisp voice from behind. They both turned to see Anastasia gliding over, teacup in hand. "Sorry to disappoint."

"I didn't mean...that is..." Champion that she was, Moira inhaled and tried again, hand outstretched. "I'm Moira Gear."

"I know all about you." Anastasia's voice had a husky tone to it that always sounded like she'd just finished having sex. If he hadn't known her, he'd have thought it part of her paramour training, but Kennerick had it too – a most bizarre family trait.

"Good things, I hope," Moira answered.

"My information comes from Kenny. So, no. As I understand it, we are to know each other well? Of course, we don't. Not yet. Patrick, go away. Do manly things and leave us two birds alone." Anastasia stood by the door, clearly not willing to move until he did.

He could be just as stubborn. "We came here to get her changed. That's all, Anna. I can't have a woman coming in and out of my house. I thought we might borrow some clothes for her and—"

"And these are all things that women do alone. She's in good hands, Clock. If you want my assistance, I'll need to speak with this woman alone. I promise to give her back, but I'll have her account of this without your interference."

The woman had a nasty habit of saying exactly what she meant. He may have had a chance, but Moira's face had gone from shocked to intrigued.

Well, hell.

He didn't want the women alone. God knows what Anastasia would say. She could be circumspect when decorum demanded it, but Kennerick's sister never had a good grasp of when and where that was.

"Is there a problem, Clock? I've trusted Clocks with my most prized possession for years and yet you can't spare Ms. Gear's company for—"

"That's enough. Look—"

Moira cut him off with a wicked grin. "I think that'd be a lovely idea."

"Traitor."

She shrugged and took a step toward Anastasia. "As lovely as the company in your home has been, I'd love to spend some time with my own kind. We have some things to discuss."

"Such as?"

No response.

This wouldn't end well, but expressly forbidding her to leave would have similarly disastrous results. "You'll talk about me the entire time."

"You aren't that important," Moira said, with a mischievous laugh in her throat.

"Is that anyway to speak to the man you intend to marry?"

"Marry!" Anastasia clutched her chest. A little heavy on the theatrics, but he couldn't discount the shock in her eyes. "No wonder my brother was in such a frenzy to meet for dinner this evening. It's settled. Go. We'll chatter about you all morning and well past lunch. There's nothing to else to be done. We've a wedding to discuss."

Three minutes later, he was out on his arse with the door slammed shut behind him. He tried to be superior about the whole thing. He couldn't well drag her out, and it wasn't as if he didn't have work to do.

Patrick got on his bicycle and, after a sickening number of backward glances, pedaled off. He found a somewhat secluded viewing area in one of the recreational tunnels. The systems here blew a breeze fast enough to lift his coattails. Maybe it would blow the pieces of his mind to resolutions of their varied investigations. He'd bring Moira here one day, but for now, he found a spot near the cutty reefs and pulled out his small book of notations from his pocket.

To get this over and done with, to get on with his life, he needed to get back down to basics and focus on one case at a time.

McCoy. That had to be the easiest. And it was. The boy was still making charges and withdrawals and, by all accounts, not under duress. Assuming the name and the man doing all this were one in the same.

But then, they must be.

Each and every place someone named Samuel McCoy had gone was a place that catered to the middle and upper classes. No one could fake that. Not easily. It had taken Anastasia years to meld into certain social circles, and she still slipped up once a high tide or two. This was someone who knew so much of the rules that they flittered below anyone's detection in the way that only old money could.

That meant Sam McCoy still lived. More, it established a pattern. The prat had a standard of living and was in need of currency. Lots of it.

Had he fallen into puffer ink? The drug laid men out for days at a time. But if Samuel was so bad off that he required as much money as he'd stolen, he wouldn't have been in any condition to fool anyone.

Gambling then?

Far more likely.

Patrick made a quick list of the gaming halls in nearby tunnels and hubs. He'd tick them off one by one and, with Moira occupied, he'd find no better time.

Heart racing with the red energy that accompanied breakthroughs, he jumped to his feet, only to find his bicycle in someone else's grubby hands.

The little thief struggled under the weight of it before giving up and dashing through the crowd of strolling ladies and squealing children at play. Patrick didn't let the scoundrel out of his sight, coming up on him at the gate, just before he would have been able to blend into the traffic of the greater tunnels.

His hand slipped on the boy's sweat-drenched collar twice before getting a solid grip on the lad. The boy grunted and twisted, refusing to go easy.

Women screamed behind him and he thought he heard the swish of falling dresses and the sighs of well-practiced faints. More importantly, a policeman's whistle trilled, but it was soon overcome by the wheezing, hacking cough of its owner. "Caught one? Eh, you're Clock, the investigator? Pleasure's mine. All mine. You know, half the department wants to hire you?"

He tried in vain to ignore the thrill of validation. After all these years, it meant something to be not a Clock but *The* Clock. It wasn't Matron's title anymore, but his. He'd never take the job with the police department – not unless Moira changed her mind and money started to drain – but damn, it felt good to know that he could.

"It's not bad to hear you say that officer. As for our little thief, he tried to nick my—"

"I saw, I saw. Just on the other side of the park," the man said between wheezes. He whipped out a motley kerchief and dabbed at his glistening temples. "I'll handle it from here."

"No doubt."

Patrick waited for the man to realize that he indeed could not. The officer was on his cycle with no partner and no wagon in sight. Either he would have to put the lad on the machine and risk the boy pedaling away or ride it and hope the child followed. Most officers carried tethers, but in this traffic, the boy, a friend or even a stranger eager to stick it to one of the authorities would surely cut the rope binding him.

So much for following his leads.

"Look, I'll go with you and make my statement now. It'll save me a trip." The flush-faced officer snapped the bait and soon he pushed one cycle with each hand, while Patrick kept a grip on the boy.

They didn't go unnoticed. Beleaguered vendors shot looks of approval, but he knew there were other eyes too. The kind that hid in shadow and looked for opportunities to strike. Associates of the boy or others hoping to avoid the gaze of the officer? He wasn't sure and picked up the pace, eager to shake off the tingling sensation of being watched. Truly watched. So much so that he started planning his escape. If it came to it, he'd force the boy down with one hand while reaching for his blade with the other. It was a long line of hope, but it'd have to work. The officer certainly wouldn't be of much assistance.

Every so often, he'd look down at the small face. Tiny, but hard and leathered from the savagery that orphaned life required for survival. This last time, he caught the lad grinning and tightened his grip on the clammy, small wrist.

"Almost there."

"Good." Twice already, the boy had tried to break free. He'd been certain the boy had some help – an unseen hand yanking through the bodies. And yet each time he turned, Patrick only saw more faces. Innocent faces.

He didn't relax until they walked through the glass doors of the municipal building. The officer took him to a holding cell while Patrick waited to give his testimony of events.

Five minutes passed.

To keep from going insane, he stared out the window at the people going about their day below. They all had the same glacial smiles – the great façade of London. How many of these men struggled under the weight of a family name as he did? Or worse, ached for the approval of someone unable to give it?

He'd tried to live his professional life as Matron...as Grandma...had taught him, but with Moira now on the stage, he'd steered the sub well aground.

Still, he knew deep inside that Grandma would have been pleased.

It took a full fifteen minutes of staring out the pane for him to get it through his thick skull. Matron raised a man, not a voiceless mimic. She'd raised him to think for himself. To reason.

And to decide.

And he'd decided on Moira.

Those air-emptying fifteen minutes had a far opposite effect on the officer. The man returned a snarling, stomping caricature of his former self. "Talk."

"Is something the matter?"

"You were in the park when..."

"In the park reviewing my notes when I looked up to find my bicycle in his hands. He tried to make off with it, but I caught him. That's when you showed up."

"Right. Write that. Sign this. I'll be back."

And another ten minutes ticked away, along with Patrick's good nature. He damn near balled the paper and shoved it in his chest when the officer waddled back though the double doors. "Here's the testimony."

"Thanks. For the good it'll do."

"Meaning?"

"The boy's already bailed out."

"What? How? It's Hellion, isn't it? He's the only man with the money and motivation to get it done."

But the officer shook his head. "Some richie named Sammie McCoy. You know him?"

He didn't answer. No time. Patrick ran to catch the precious link in his case, pushing through the officers and fighting his way to the streets. And only then, only at the bottom of the stairs as he looked out on wagons and bicycles full of people, did he realize he'd never catch up with the pair. Just like that, the crowded tunnels swallowed had them whole. "Samuel McCoy is Hellion."

"No he ain't." Patrick twisted to see the now wheezing officer who took another lung-whistling breath before continuing. "After your meeting with the captain the other day, he led a special force investigating Hellion. He's Chinese. We know the bastard's name as well. Tim Hilkreel is Lord Hellion. Charges for kidnapping and murder are being drawn as we speak."

"But what does that have to do with McCoy?"

"Not my problem." The officer shrugged and ambled back up the steps, disappearing behind the gilded doors of the station.

But this was all wrong.

Even more, too convenient.

Chapter XI

Anastasia matched her home as if she'd been born from the golden carpets and plush, burgundy curtains. Her dress was the color of the sun at shore and every fold pressed to a razor's edge. Ribbons and sea vines entwined in her dark tresses set off the sparkles of her seafoam-blue eyes. "If you are in an indelicate situation, I can help."

"I don't understand. Patrick has been the most gracious of hosts."

"I'm sure he has. I'm not one to judge. Do as you do, I always say, but...are you..."

"Yes?"

The question hung in the air between them and Moira was perfectly willing to let it hang right there until the woman started making sense. She had no idea what Ms. Anastasia went on about, but the woman looked positively giddy.

Moira had a few questions of her own. "So, Ms. Clock—"

"No. That isn't my last name and please, call me Anastasia."

Hmm. A hesitation in divulging her family name. She had to have one and it'd be easily discovered. So why not tell her? She was being toyed with. Or tested. Perhaps both.

"I have to thank you for all that you've done to help me. You see, the truth of the matter is, I've come here to solve an investigation."

"So you're not marrying Patrick?"

"I am."

"Ah. A marriage of the minds then?"

"Quite."

"And the investigation?"

"Children have gone missing and no one seems to notice."

"But you do?"

She leaned in, grabbed a daily laid upon the table and waved it in the air. "They show up in the papers. No names, no markers of identification. No one cares because they're from the lower tunnels. Months of this. Months and no one stops it. I will. We will."

It was as if someone vented a tunnel and released a metric ton of pressure. Anastasia's smile deepened, the corner of her eyes relaxed and she leaned back into her chair. "How can I help?"

"If you hear anything—"

"I'll have my girls keep an ear to the men. If they hear word of this, you'll know. He likes you, you know?"

"Patrick?"

"Of course, dear. But I meant my brother. He didn't at first, but his tone has changed. I haven't the details of what you did or what precisely changed, but it has. That's no small feat."

"Kennerick is..."

"A difficult, presumptuous ass and I love him for it."

She'd heard the words before, but never from a woman and certainly not about their own family. She hid her grin behind the offered cup of tea. "He's very direct."

"He's an ass."

"I didn't mean—"

"Moira, I want us to be dear friends and that requires openness. You know what I am and you know what I do. I know that you're living under the same roof with a man not your husband. I'm offering myself as an alibi for who knows what. Two, as it goes. Can't we at least speak plainly with one another?"

True. True and true. "Are you sure?"

"Of course. You're practically family."

"Teach me how to make love."

Anastasia's teacup crashed to the floor. The maid hovering outside the door, and who ought to come clean it up, collapsed into a fit of giggles. No, not giggles. Loud-mouthed, stomach-clutching cackles.

You could heat a kettle with the warmth flooding to her face, but she kept her gaze straight, locked on Anastasia. The woman said she wanted plain speech. There is was. Now if she could just find a blanket to hide under.

"Not an indelicate situation then?"

"Sorry?"

"Child, girl. I'm asking if you're with child."

"No. No, no. We haven't uh…well…hence the question."

Anastasia's pearly white teeth clamped down on scandalously painted lips. "This is good. Better than I thought."

"I hadn't asked for your amusement. I'll pay."

Anastasia's wavy curls shook from side to side. "You won't. We're family. And I meant every word of what I said. To have a man who appreciates your work, Moira, is a blessing. I thought I had it once. He couldn't take it in the end."

"I'm sorry."

"Don't be. I'm richer now. It helps. The point is, I hope this works for you. I hope you keep this."

"So you'll help me?"

"Help? Honey, I'll show you." Anastasia stood up, arms extended and calling for the still recovering maid. "Sally, you be the bloke. Moira, get over here and lay down."

"You can't be serious."

"Of course I am. I'll not have it said that one of my girls can't do the job."

"One of your—"

"Do you want my help or not?"

It wasn't a question of wants but of needs. Where else would she get this information? Not her mother, for sure. She would take this logically, treating it as any problem needing to be solved. She'd asked for help and now she was getting it. She wasn't a true beginner, so there couldn't be much to learn. "I know how to kiss."

"Who taught you?"

"Patrick. Well, of sorts. I'm a quick study."

"Let's expand up the basics then. Do you feel him? His tongue?"

"Yes."

"And do you return the favor?"

"Y...yes."

"Good."

"Sally? Here. Now. Moira, put your arm around her neck."

"I do that already."

Anastasia shot her an appreciative wink. "Nice girl and put your other hand around Sally's lower waist, just above her hip."

"This hardly seems regular."

"None of this is, honey. Arm. Waist. Good. This is how you properly kiss a man. Let him in. When you close him in physically, he understands that there's no one else in the world that matters. There's no room for even the hint of another man to enter this locked space of yours."

"I feel as though I should write this down."

"This? Dear girl, we're just getting started. Now the first time he takes you to bed..."

He returned to Anastasia's door more confused than when he'd left. Every time he made headway, something kicked him back a stroke. He needed Moira. She'd get it sorted. Her mind saw things his missed, and he smiled at the glimpse of their future as partners in every sense of the word. Seeing her face ought to brighten his mood.

He just hadn't expected it to look like that.

She had painted cheekbones and..."What did you do to your eyes?"

Moira reached up to the space between her brows. "Anastasia is a wonder with a bit of string. Still stings though."

"And she gave you clothes?"

Moira fluffed the bottom of her green and golden dress, then entwined her arm in his. "A few. Anastasia had the rest sent over already."

"Speaking of, where is she? And the staff? Why are you answering the door?"

"Gone. She and Kennerick went out to the theatre and all the girls are busy."

"He hates the theatre."

"Life is an exploration of new experiences. Are we walking or riding?"

"We need a carriage. I can't take you home like this in full view of the street."

"You make too much of it, Patrick. People will think I'm a client of yours."

Dressed like that, they'd probably think he was a client of hers. "Moira—"

"Please, Patrick?"

"But are cycles are—"

"I think we should walk."

"What sense does that make? I'll just have to come back for the bicycles tomorrow."

"Lovely night, isn't?" She scooted ahead of him and down the steps of the row house. "The lightning fish are expected to swarm tonight. Maybe we'll spot their flashes on the walk back."

He couldn't say that she had to pull him. His big ol' desperate feet went right along on their own at her command. She talked of nothing and yet every observation, from the artificial bioluminescent street lamps to the rising cost of snails, had his full attention. "This isn't like you, Moira."

"What?"

"This. This small talk."

"I can speak of more than victims and mayhem. When we're married, we'll have to find more to discuss."

"Slugs, for instance?"

"Not slugs. Snails. Slug costs haven't changed. It really is a lovely night."

"Right. Invertebrates aside, things got a lot more interesting later in the day. Are we allowed to speak about work?"

"Did you solve one of the cases?"

"No."

"Then not tonight," she said.

"How about things tangentially connected to work?"

"No. You're going to either look up and hope for lightning fish or you can look at me."

He tripped over the curb, recovering fast enough to avoid future embarrassment by way of a full fall. "Look?"

Moira rocked on her heels and went in for the kill. "You haven't mentioned how I look."

"Beautiful."

"Thank you. Mind this next step."

She chattered the rest of the way, stopping to breathe when they reached the tunnel they called home. Such a strange confusion of words: *they* and *home*.

He lied to himself that the late hour required a lot less caution. No one respectable would be about. It was that hour when lovers scrambled from one bed to another. Still, he was determined to shield her as much as he could.

They ducked in through the back alley that doubled as a lane for water and sewage pipes between property lines. The homes on both sides of it, his included, were walled off for privacy and additional protection. Hoisting her over was not the worst thing he'd ever done. Moira had plenty of space in the back for him to grip, and she further rewarded him with a series of grunts and moans in exertion.

He'd make her moan for him again under better circumstances one day. For now, he had to concentrate on getting over this wall himself. Matron Clock believed in two things: plans and redundancies. In the eventuality of a running approach, she'd constructed several secret paths to enter the property. This was his least favorite.

Into the rear guard wall were carved a series of grooves for foot- and handholds. One wrong step would send you crashing to the ground.

He only did it once.

This time.

Perhaps it was Moira's cut-off scream that caught him so off guard to cause the incident. He stumbled over the ledge and there she was, trundled up in fishing netting and hanging from the side of the house, several feet above the ground.

She worked as she spoke, cutting the ropes with the knife he'd given her back when she still was half woman, half curiosity. Not that much had changed. "Can I attribute this to the former lady of the house?"

"You can," he said, joining his knife to the task. "You're handling this remarkably well."

"Thank you. How many more of these traps can I expect to find?"

"Get cutting. We'll do a walkthrough soon. For this month, we'll focus on the first floor."

One of Moira's legs slid through some space in the netting. She rocked back and forth as if on a swing. Moira stopped sawing to use her knife as a pointer. "We'd best err on the side of caution. You'll have to carry me everywhere in the interest of safety."

"Starting now," he said, releasing the last binding and catching her before she tumbled all the way down. He cradled her in front of him, arms under her cushy backside. One of her hands came to rest around his neck, and despite the obvious benefits, it really was for the better.

While the front door was relatively straightforward, the back was riddled with clever surprises. One had to know the exact place to step or risk a pain-laced welcome. He ought to have gone over this with her before, but he'd expected her stay to be temporary. Somewhere between then and now, this old building had changed from his house to their home.

His heart had changed too.

What little portion that remained of the small, beating thing was now consumed with her. One day he should tell her that. For now, she needed to be just a business deal. No problem.

Moira tucked her head in the crook of his neck and he sucked in air as she laid soft kisses against his throat.

Problem.

"Moira?"

"I missed you."

"Moira."

"You taste like the sea."

Really? Because he could almost taste her father's fist. "I should tell you to stop."

"You tried that once before."

"I should try again."

"That would be an unsuccessful venture." Her lips traveled higher and he'd be damned if her tongue didn't dart out and trace the outline of his jaw.

"What exactly did you and Anastasia talk about?"

"Things."

"Such as?"

She licked...*licked*... his bottom lip. "Good things."

He held back long enough to get her inside the house but didn't make it much further. Patrick dropped her legs, pushed her against the back of the door and kissed her as he'd wanted to from the moment he'd met her.

One hand latched around his neck, the other, his waist, pulling him closer to her body. She kissed as if they were lovers already, pressing her whole body into his, yielding her mouth to him while still controlling his pace with her hand on his back.

He needed to stop this, but his legs moved on their own, carrying them both upstairs and to her bedroom door.

"Stay with me tonight, Patrick."

"Do you know what you're asking?"

"I do," she said chuckling against his chest.

"This isn't a game."

"I know that."

"If I come in, there's no going back. This line we've been playing around will be crossed. Right now, as of this moment, either of us can still walk away."

One small hand slipped between them and all good sense vanished as she grabbed hold of his manhood through his trousers. "Does this feel like a game to you?"

Tomorrow he'd throttle or thank Anastasia, but tonight, he'd enjoy Moira. "I won't leave you any quarter to regret this."

"I know. That's why I'm here." She pushed his arms off hers, walked around him and stepped inside her bedroom. "Help me undress."

Good God.

His clumsy fingers worked unending rows of buttons. Each layer shed exposed new and magnificent expanses of flesh. Her body was perfect. The curves hinted at during the day held their own under his greedy eyes at night. With the laces undone and clothes piled at their feet, she turned around to face him.

Really, face him. Head on, chin out and unblinking.

"Unclench your jaw, little warrior. I'm here and not going anywhere, unless you tell me to."

"I'm not scared, Patrick."

"You never should be. Don't you know you hold reign over me? That all control rests in your hands?"

"So undress."

He did. And still, she did not turn or avert her eyes.

"Kiss my hand."

He did.

"Kiss my knee."

He did.

"And kiss me...here," she said, pointing to the tuft of hair between her legs.

He started at her thighs, head dizzy with the scent of her. He didn't so much kiss as lick, dragging his tongue up the inside of her leg until the damp hairs of her grotto danced across the bridge of his nose.

Then he did as she commanded, spreading open her lips and bathing her with his mouth. Spicy. Salty and with her own unique flavor of tartness. He'd have laughed if he had the air to spare, but everything about her left him shattered and breathless. He went back for a second helping. "Is this all right?"

"Very all right," she said in an equally ragged voice.

"Then sit on the bed so I can get a proper taste."

She laid back, legs dangling off the edge...and his tongue dangling between them. She let out soft mewing sounds, and though she no longer touched him *there* physically, it had the same effect.

He could take her now, she was ready, but he enjoyed her. And enjoyed watching her enjoy him. Moira twisted and moaned beneath his mouth, speaking nonsensical things that had him smiling.

That turned at the realization that he was about to cause her great pain. He'd never had a virgin before, but had heard enough to temper himself and his expectations. He'd go slow or die trying.

Then she slid off the side of the bed, straddled him, and he realized he might actually die. The woman kissed him with passion that set his lips on fire and her hands, those wonderful wicked things, went down to his aching cock. He beat out a gruff, "Don't."

"Why?"

"I can't take it."

"You can."

She stroked and pulled and tugged and jerked until his temples throbbed and he dropped his head to her neck. "Please, Moira. You have to stop."

"No. I like you like this. At my command."

Her second hand joined in and he was done for. The tightly wound locks that held him in check were rent apart. His release came hard and fast, spilling between the two of them. He took the next few seconds gathering his breath and hunting for the right things to say. How the hell to explain this to a virgin? When he opened his mouth to try, she kissed him again and giggled. "It tastes different than I imagined it would."

"Tell me you didn't..."

"It got on my hand."

"You're killing me..."

"Patrick?" He pulled back to see her nibbling a crooked finger and halfway grinning. "I'm ready."

"I'm not. Give a man a minute. What's his name?"

"Who?"

"The man who taught you to do that?"

"Why?"

"So I can kill him."

"He is a she. Anastasia. Still want to kill her?"

"Depends on how she taught you. Come here." He didn't think it possible, but already he was ready for her, needing to feel her body over his, covering him in the most intimate way. He wrapped one luscious leg behind his back and splayed open the other with a gentle push at the side of her knee. "It may be uncomfortable this first time, but I swear to you Moira, I will bring you pleasure every day of your life."

He raised up, tilted her hips and—

A crash and howl from downstairs had them both scrambling for their clothes. The screaming below turned to curses and all flung at his direction. "Stay here."

"No."

"Yes, Moira! My house, my rules."

"Exactly. My house. My rules."

She had him. He couldn't very well tell her *not yet* when he was treating her like a wife seconds earlier. But damn it, this was an issue of safety, not pride or disrespect. "That is not Kennerick."

"I picked up that much."

"I won't have you hurt."

"Then we are in agreement." She produced the knife from her pile of clothes. "I won't have me hurt either. Lace me up."

And so it was they went down to investigate together with him fighting all the way to at least keep her half protected behind him.

The house had a remarkable way of turning predators to prey, and theirs lay strung upside-down by one leg a few steps from the cane rack. The man, clearly from Asian waters, looked youngish – though older than himself and maybe even Anastasia.

And breaking into his house.

He knew but one man who could possible fit that description. "Lord Hellion, I presume?"

"King."

"Seems a big grandiose."

"I am grand and at your service," he said, with his version of an upside-down bow. He pointed to the rope about his feet. "If you'd be so kind?"

"Certainly. A word first, if you don't mind. Since we're being so polite. Might I ask what you're doing in my home?"

"Hanging from your roof."

"Quite. Might I ask why?"

"Ahh, that. Yes, well, I thought it was time we met. Word on the street is that you and some woman, that one I reckon, are trying to solve the mystery of the lost boys."

"And you mean to stop us?"

"Quite the contrary. Really, I'm starting to see stars. Down, please."

"Keep talking."

Hellion smacked his lips and sucked in air between slightly gapped teeth. "Further, the mood of the tunnel implies that I have something to do with this."

"And you claim this is in error?" Moira asked beside him.

King Hellion's eyes cut to her in open measurement. "You missed a button. No. I have nothing to do with this at all. In fact, seven of those boys were mine. You're going to help me get them back."

"Why should I believe you?"

"I'm in your bloody house!"

"Hanging from the ceiling," Patrick corrected.

"Immaterial! I sought you out – no weapons in hand."

Moira elbowed him and he followed her gaze to two knives glistening on the floor. Hellion didn't grin. He didn't smirk. He didn't do anything other than yawn. "Well, they're not in hand. Please?"

The man wouldn't do any good to them passed out. "If you try anything—"

"You'll do something terrible like kill me or pry off my toenails, yes, I've heard it all before. But we have a mystery to solve, and for that I am willing to come to you." The man didn't say anything else until he was upright. Hellion pulled at the white cuffs of his tailored, pinstriped suit and cracked his neck. "I'll pay you."

"Damn straight you will. The sitting room's this way. Moira, bring your tools. I need to remember this."

King Hellion took the seat nearest the door and started talking. He named the missing children, their ages and descriptions. He paused when Moira walked in with a nod but resumed his long list of information. Patrick half expected the criminal to bring up her presence, but he didn't, save a few quizzical glances now and then.

At least, until the end. "What is she doing?"

"She can hear you," Moira said, graphite dragging across the cream-colored page.

"She's quite bold."

"Said the thief," answered Moira in her still-dry voice. But if she had one weakness, it was her drawings, and she got up to show Hellion her handiwork. The man's gasp brought back memories of his own, the first time he'd seen her magic. But something in his eyes looked off and he scrunched up his face.

Hellion pointed near the top. "Tim Hilkreel. Who's that?"

"We know your real name, Hellion," she said, lips pursed in wry amusement.

"Unless you're my mother, you don't. Do I look like someone named Hilkreel, lady?"

Patrick kicked the leg of Hellion's chair. "Watch your mouth. You've said your piece. I don't know that I believe any of it, but if what you say checks out, we'll be in touch. How will I find you?"

"You won't. Bring my boys back and you'll get what you deserve."

"And if I don't come through?"

Hellion shrugged and made his way to the hall, not bothering to turn around as he reached for the door. "You'll get what you deserve."

Moira shivered next to him as the thin man disappeared into the night. "I don't appreciate threats."

"You have nothing to be afraid of. I won't let anyone hurt you." He wrapped his arm around her and led her away.

"I know that. But I still don't appreciate it, nor the interruption of your seduction."

"My seduction?"

"Mmmhmm. See, tomorrow, we need to discover if that man just told us the truth. There's nothing we can do about it tonight, so perhaps—"

His lips shut her up. His arms picked her up. And she lifted him in all the right places. He didn't even pretend to want to leave her in her bedroom, instead taking her straight to his. He undressed her slowly this time, still eager, but with a little more control than earlier in the night. When he placed her in the center of his bed, he knew she belonged there and that she'd never leave that spot again. She was his starting now and not ending until the end of forever.

Chapter XII

She woke up sore on the inside and smiling from ear to ear. Her face darn near cracked from it.

Had they...?

Yes.

Had she...?

Oh, yes.

She owed Anastasia her thanks along buckets and buckets gold. She'd been right on all counts. Yes, it had hurt a little, but his mouth down there more than made up for it.

Her stomach fluttered at the memory of what he'd done, how he'd so filled her completely, stretching her body to accommodate his.

Wicked juices. That's what Anastasia had called them, and they flowed at the sheer memory of it all. She rolled over to find him smiling at her. "Good morning."

His rough finger traced the outline of her chin. "How are you feeling?"

"Wicked."

"Aye. I'd kiss you, but it'd lead to more of what happened last night."

"Is that a bad thing?"

"I need to get you back to your room before Ken—"

"Our good Kennerick had too much to drink last night and decided to stay with his sister."

"You planned this." He dropped a wet kiss on her shoulder. "Every bit of it."

"Not *every* bit, but aren't you glad I did?"

Patrick eased his way back against the headrest. She rolled until her head was in his lap. Scarred hands drew intoxicating circles around her breast, while she smiled against his stomach. He smelled of sweat and musk and...her.

"We can catch the next submarine to London's Green Hub."

She popped up, sure she misunderstood. "Whatever for?"

"The same reason everyone else goes. We need to be married."

"Patrick—"

"Because I won't stop doing this to you. I can't stop touching you. Even as we face a damn near impossible case, instead of finding clues, I'm thinking of what I want to do to you next."

Was there more? Anastasia had hinted that certain men had certain tastes but couldn't offer up anything on Patrick. And while it was true that she wanted to discover more of him, that didn't erase her duties or responsibility to those poor children. They'd have sons of their own someday. If anything ever happened to her, she'd want someone to fight just as hard for them. "Our marriage will be the celebration for solving this case."

"So we resort to carrying on in the meantime?"

"Don't make it sound less than it is, Patrick. I'm not going anywhere. Are you?"

"You know I'm not."

"Well that's that. We won't be left with any time to work together on this if we go on with a wedding. Let alone an announced proposal. And I want a wedding – a true one. Not something hurried and unfussed. You'll give me that."

"I will."

"That wasn't a question."

"I know."

"Right. So I'm off."

"What?"

Getting out of that bed hurt. Away from his warmth, coldness wrapped about her like the ends of glaciers. *Later. Later, later.* They'd have a long future of doing this.

Of course, Patrick made his more difficult than need be. The lout pouted like a child and twice grabbed her around the middle to pull her back to bed. Only the alarm that signaled Mrs. Catherine's entry slowed his grabby hands.

The sweet but ruthlessly efficient woman would head straight to the kitchen. Moira took the opportunity to wrap a sheet around her and run to her own room. She made it.

Almost.

"Good morning, Moira."

"Kennerick."

"Beautiful morning."

"Isn't it just."

The prat leaned against his bedroom door, still wearing his clothes from last night. "My sister likes you."

"Can we discuss this another time?"

"Meaning, a time when you have clothes on?"

"I would appreciate it if—"

"We're family now. That means I'm allowed to tease you."

"And you call this teasing?"

To her great shock, the man apologized. She looked around, expecting to find a glowering Patrick in the hall, but it was just the two of them. Kennerick's head turned from side to side, then landed back on her. "What is it?"

"I just thought...you apologized."

"Yes, and I'm doing it retroactively as well."

"Um, well, thank you."

Her gave her a curt nod, pivoted and quietly shut his door behind him. What in Hades was that about? The hope that she should take it at face value didn't shrivel up and die full stop – after all, this was Kennerick – but could that have been genuine?

Anastasia *had* said that he liked her.

Her morning started good compounded upon good and thrice multiplied by good. And yet, she had bigger things – grander things on both ends of the scale to manage. She washed, quickly dressed in her brother's rags and ran downstairs, leaving a note to Patrick of her whereabouts. She wasn't about to start asking him for permission to do things. Besides, telling him would lead to a fight. She had to go out. Alone. The collection of dailies in the hidden floor of the house didn't go on forever. She needed to go further back in time, both in papers here and beyond London. There had to be more clues, more similarities, and that meant a trip to the library. No harm would come to her there.

She picked up a meatpie on the way, knowing the vendor wouldn't be here by the time she got back. She considered it a goodwill gesture and wrapped the pastry in a kerchief to deliver to Kennerick upon her return.

She tipped her head as men were wont to do and the vendor returned it with a quick, "Nice day to you, ma'am."

Oh no. She cleared her throat and prayed for a lower register to her voice, even as she knew it trembled. "Wh-what?"

The vendor flushed and his son giggled behind grimy hands. The man shushed him and nodded. "Sorry, sir. I mean to say. Don't know where me head's at."

She tried to be angry, but there was no ill will on his face. Nothing but remorse. Oh, why correct what they all knew to be true. She shrugged, thanked him in her regular voice and continued on.

Nothing stopped or slowed her pedaling after that. More determined than ever, she wove through the crowded tunnels to the four-storied downtown building. One of the biggest constructs in the city, it had one full end of a tunnel to itself. Outside, people gathered to shop for knickknacks or pose for street portrait drawers. Her goal waited inside.

Among the stacks, she found the old dailies, but nothing stood out. Sure, evidence of more missing boys, and she noted their locations, but there wasn't any identifying information.

With each newly disclosed incident, she added it to the list, along with their date of disappearance or murder.

It took a two full pages of notes before she noticed the pattern.

Their numbers were growing. The further she went back, weeks, months, the fewer missing and killed children she found, until there were none listed.

What changed?

She tried again, picking two days of the week from each month and going back in time. Searching a newspaper without knowing what you're looking for was torture.

Finding it, on the other hand, was sublime.

It didn't stand out until four months back. A large advert for workers in above-ground countries.

She checked the month after – the advert was smaller.

She then checked the month before – the advert took up the full page.

In fact, there was a direct correlation of the number of missing children to the size of this advert. When no children were gone, it was huge. Conversely, it all but disappeared in the last month of dailies.

It might be a coincidence and yet it would explain so much. Only boys had been taken. Only the healthy. Only the poor. Taken and not a single body found, save those children who'd had defensive wounds. In fact, no child had been found without them.

But they had been found drugged. Were those poor children the ones who didn't succumb?

Lists hadn't led her astray yet, so she made another one. This time, she listed the names of the companies in the adverts, grabbed her notes and headed over to the library's holdings of licensure and incorporation.

What looked like nine companies were in fact three with tentacles that stretched far beyond the borders of London.

With what Kennerick's physical examinations had produced, a terrible picture started to take shape. Hadn't he said that blown pupils indicated oxygenation drugs? Such would have been required for the long depressurization process. Boys that poor had likely never been above ground and would need weeks, if not months, to go from one depth to another. These same drugs, in the right doses, could render someone immobile.

She didn't recognize the names of the owners, but Patrick might. She also found surveyor sketches of islands and private waterways transferred to these same men within the last two years.

Moira rushed out the door with notes under each arm and shoved her discoveries in the basket on her cycle. No leisurely trip, she pedaled home, standing the whole way. When the house peered into view, she jumped off the still-moving cycle, abandoning it in the yard, and took the steps two at a time, wheezing as she made her way inside, screaming for Patrick at the top of her lungs.

The stairs above the hidden room lifted, and he stomped out from below. "Have you lost your mind? Don't leave again without telling me where you're going."

"I left a note."

"One I just found. Hellion's out there and—"

"He's not the problem. In fact, I think he was telling us the truth. All of it. Mosten, Eaton, Myles – what do these three men have in common?"

"They're city council members."

"Right. What? No...no. They own above-water properties."

"And they're all council members. What did you uncover?"

"Then it's massive. Bigger than we could have possibly imagined."

"What is?" Kennerick asked, leaning over the top railing. He was still dressed in his bedclothes, holding a bottle of whisky by the neck. "What did I miss?"

Patrick sagged against the raised steps, disbelief weighing down his voice at the horror in his hands. "Eaton, Mosten and Myles."

"I don't know 'em."

"You do, Ken."

"I don't. Wait. Mosten? I think I slept with his wife. No, sorry, his sister. She's married to Chief Detective Policeman Bane. Are they in on this?"

Both men stared, jaws on the floor, as she laid out her findings before them. When she was done, Kennerick took a huge swig of his drink, came down and handed Patrick the bottle. Her intended drank for a straight five seconds. Since neither man appeared capable of continued speech, she picked up the slack. "Which leaves us with this question: How does one turn in the authorities to the authorities?"

"I need to pay a visit to Bane."

Kennerick shook his head. "That's a death wish."

"He's right, Patrick."

"I'm not a fool, and it's our best chance. We can't bring this up without tangible proof. If we're right, those children are still here. At least some of them. Depressurization would take ages."

"So we search the hubs for those with access to long-term holding chambers," Kennerick added.

"No," she said. "A bunch of poor children in long-term depressurization? That would get noticed. They need to be rich enough to have private facilities. Which removes the chief somewhat, but the brother-in-law is still in play."

Patrick grunted an agreement. "But they'd need him to ensure the blind eye of the police. With him being family, they could trust him. The man offered me a job. I think I owe it to him to hear what he has to say."

"Not now – it's too late in the afternoon. The three of us ought to get our turtles in a row before taking one more step."

And thus, it started. Instead of spending another night wrapped in one man's arms, she spent it with her back aching and bent over stacks of files and lists. She read until her eyes crossed and the words blurred together, fading into darkness.

Twice, she drifted off, but when she woke up the third time, she was in Patrick's arms being carried upstairs. "Perhaps I'm not the best investigator," she managed to get out between yawns.

"Don't be silly. If not for your pigheadedness, we'd have never even started. You may well be the best of us."

"Patrick, my bedroom's the other way."

"Is it now?"

"You're staying?"

His shaking head did the craziest things to her. Pride, shame, loss and love – four emotions from a single action.

"I need to help Kennerick," he said. "But I want you here when I return."

"I know."

"I'd rather be here."

"I know that too and I love you for—"

"Love?"

"Well, I—" and whatever else she meant to say didn't matter against his lips. So yes, he did stay a while longer than expected and yes, he later returned downstairs and yes, she did love him for doing both.

Chapter XIII

Chief Detective Policeman Bane rapped his billy stick across the new desk and winked. Crumbs from what must have been lunch littered his beard, and he hacked into a brown-crusted kerchief pulled from a squeaky top drawer. Behind him was a wall of books. Strange what'll shock you. He never figured Bane bright enough for some of the classics stored on his shelves. "That's new."

Bane jerked his thumb towards the collection. "You like it? We took out one of the walls to open it up a bit. A big man like me needs a big office."

So, not a reader, just a show-off. "Bane, the relationship between my family and the force goes way back, and I've been thinking about a more lasting agreement."

"I knew it. You have it in you, man. You're just about the best of us. I'll not lie. It's been better than good having a bloke on the outside."

"There are places I can go, questions I can ask without a badge."

"Exactly." Bane sat down and moved a stack of papers from one side to the other. "You'll be bogged down in reports if I hire you. Never mind the pay – it won't be nearly enough. But something on the side, perhaps? I'm sure the council can find some discretionary funds."

"I look forward to hearing the terms."

"You can do something to improve them before we reach the negotiation table. Find Hellion. We've let that man run long enough. You bring him to me and I promise the reward will be handsome."

"Consider it done."

Bane rocked back in his chair and yelled at his office boy for more tea. The lad's stool scraped across the floor as he hurried away. "Let's see how long it takes the stupid bastard this time."

"Part of the public works campaign? I hear that some of the children are doing quite well."

Bane's face twisted and darkened at the mention of the crusade – a movement to place underserved youth in apprenticeships with hopes of brighter futures. It got them out of the dark tunnels and into homes at night. For their employers, it provided free labor. Bane, however, looked at the boy's empty seat and sneered. "Rubbish. I came up the hard way. Worked for what I got."

Married up was more like it, but Patrick kept his trap shut. People always talked themselves into confession if you were willing to let them go on long enough.

"Now these little turds get a pass straight though. Stupid program, but it makes the council look good."

"And you as well, Chief Detective."

"And that's the only reason, I'll tell you that. Council says we need to push that it works. I suppose I'm willing to deal with it. Anything to get them off tunnels. If we didn't do this, they'd spend the whole damned day running around, causing trouble. Best they go somewhere."

"Agreed."

Bane's eyes narrowed and he scratched at his beard, ignoring the crumbs that drifted to the paper below. "I wasn't sure how to take you for a good long while, Clock. Now I think I'm beginning to see the light of things. Tell you what. There's an event tonight. I know it's short notice, but it's a nice to-do with all the people that matter in London. The best from every hub. You should come. I think they'll want to meet their investment. I'm sure Miss Moira will enjoy it. Unless you're otherwise engaged..."

"I can't think of a single place we'd rather be."

Moira peered out of her bedroom window, straight into the eyes of Mrs. Huxton across the way. She didn't know who dipped behind their curtains first, but with her hair down and in a very obvious nightdress, she scrambled away, got properly dressed and headed downstairs.

Patrick had left early and she had no desire to work in the hidden room alone. She'd needed a good sleeping in anyway, and now refreshed, she set about exploring the library. Kennerick was there, rustling through pages of anatomy books. He looked and held open a page displaying a dissected heart. "You can do this better. We'd have to publish it under your initials and I'd want half the profit for shopping it around, but—"

"You'd get twenty percent, if I were interested. I'm not."

"Just think about it." He pointed to her pants. "Why are you a boy today? Going somewhere?"

"I think Huxton saw me." Well, *knew* Huxton saw her. "I'm not sure how much she made out. I thought I might do a bit of menial labor outside to throw her off. At least pretend to."

Kennerick snorted and flipped to another page in the book. "I wouldn't do it for less than forty. You had a message at the post. Who's Michael?"

"None of your business. I'll take the letter, if you please."

"I love Patrick."

"Sorry?"

Kennerick set down the book and stood up to lean against the side of the table. "I love him. He and Annie are the only things that matter to me in this shitty world. If you hurt him, if you break his heart, I will kill you and not think twice about it."

"Are you threatening me?"

"Take it how you want. Who is Michael?"

"My brother!"

Kennerick blinked once. Then again before producing the letter. "Hell, you should have just said that. Catherine's not here today. Mind making a cuppa?"

"Yes, I do." She snatched the letter from his fingers. "You just threatened me with certain death and now you want me to make you tea?"

"I took it back."

"No, you didn't."

"Fine. I take it back. Can I have—"

"If you're about to ask for tea, I'll slap you."

His mouth slammed shut and he wrinkled his face. "He's never done this before."

"Done what?"

"This," he said, pointing to her. "He's never cared. Never had his heart broken. I won't let you be the first."

She heard it there at the end – his voice caught on a memory, breaking it just a little. "Who was she? The woman who hurt you?"

Kennerick snorted and looked at the ceiling. "Trouble, but this isn't my story. It's his and yours."

"Will you tell me about her one day?"

"No."

"I see. I won't hurt him, Kennerick. I promise you that much."

"What's in the letter?"

"Still none of your business. I could do with a cup of tea while I read it, though."

"You cheeky little tart." Laughter followed him out of the room. Gracious. She'd never, ever understand the mercurial man. Or his sister for that matter. But what happened here gave her hope that one day she might, and her heart was lighter for it.

A good thing. Especially considering the contents of the note. That fact that it came from her brother and *not* her father should have been the first clue. He wanted her home.

Now.

Mother wasn't eating. Father wasn't talking. And Michael was getting blamed for indulging her, having let her review some of his old case notes.

He'd also intercepted her letter. For her own sake, he said. If Father knew where she was, he'd come down and drag her out of it. His suggestion? Lie. And if what she'd sent in the letter was already a lie, then come up with a better one. One that had her helping the homeless in far-off nations or something similar. But this, according to Michael, wouldn't swim.

She'd prove wrong every single man who doubted her.

Chest aching, hands shaking, she started penning a return note...the first of three.

To Michael, sod off. She'd return to that one later. Maybe.

To her mother, a reconfirmation of the supreme love she felt for the woman and a note of happiness and love, found with Patrick. She futzed a little with the particulars, drawing in more Anastasia and less living-and-sleeping-with-a-man, but made clear that marriage was a foregone conclusion and pushed her to start choosing dates and drawing up invitations.

The letter to her father was the easiest of all – an updated declaration of facts from the previous missive. She went a wee heavy on the intrigue, though, stating that the case had reached a head and she couldn't say more, not yet, as eyes were watching. That should knock him back.

She rose, bracing for long-distance battle via correspondence, but a smiling Kennerick holding a tea tray blocked her egress. *That* was worth sitting back down for. He didn't say anything, merely placed the service on the desk, unfolded the daily and started reading.

"Anything interesting?" she asked, pouring, savoring the absurdity of the moment.

"No missing children. No thefts. Just parties and marriage announcements. Yours curiously absent."

"Nothing so curious about it." She stopped talking at Patrick's heavy steps on the landing. With each clomp of his foot, her heart jumped and her insides tizzied. Her mind went to one thing – their thing – and for the hundredth time she wondered how people could share such a wonderful closeness at night and go about their lives in the day.

"He can finish mine," Kennerick said, standing up before Patrick even entered the room. "Those letters, you want me to post them?"

"You don't mind?"

"Of course I do. But I'm not going to sit here and watch you two stare at each other."

"What about the investigation?"

"What about it?" Patrick asked from the door. He wore a brown suit today, one with silver buttons gleaming down the front of his vest. He hung his jacket on the hook and stared at her long enough for Kennerick to grunt. Patrick shot him a glare, cleared his throat and started over. "Right. The investigation has taken a new turn. Ken, see if Anastasia can come over. We need a cover."

"For?"

"A party. Tonight. I've been invited by Bane. I need your sister to accompany us out of the house."

"Just out of the house? She's going to want to go and so will I."

"Kennerick, this is no time for games. Hopefully we can get to know these people and get them to reveal something. I'm not sure I want you—"

"All those lonely wives will need some attention," Kennerick said and drifted towards the door. "I'm going." He nearly made it, but Patrick's long arms caught him around the shoulder.

"No, I need you somewhere else. Lots of somewhere elses. If the people we're investigating are dancing, it means that they're not sleeping in their beds or working at their desks."

"And you want me to get into their homes?"

"It is your specialty."

"Was, and many years ago. And flitting things from pockets is a mite different than breaking into someone's home."

"We're too damned close—"

"The servants will be too. Something like this takes time and planning. You're mad if you expect me to go rushing into an unknown home while you spend the night dancing and drinking. I've been in irons before and I'll be damned if I let you send me back."

"Stop."

Both men turned towards her, fingers still pointed to one another in half fighting stance.

"We're being stupid. Think, boys. We can't get into any home that we haven't been invited into and so we won't. We won't break into any home at all. We'll walk right in, just as we're meant to. Patrick and I will meet and talk with the good people of the city. You and your sister will accidently find your way upstairs. It'll take all of us to do this."

Patrick's hands dropped to his hips. He did a slow look from her to Kennerick. "I told you she was good."

"I am. Now, Kennerick, please beg your sister to help."

"Done. And lady, that bicycle?"

"Yes?"

"If we manage to get out of this, consider it paid for."

In his wake, Patrick joined her at the table, scooting his chair close. He didn't sit down – not yet – not without placing a kiss on her cheek and running a finger across her exposed collarbone. "Are you all right? No pain?"

"No." A slight and wonderful lie. There was a dull ache when she climbed steps or bent to reach for something. It didn't hurt, so much. More of a reminder of what was, what they'd done and what her future held. "My brother wrote and he's not pleased."

He waved an envelope pulled from his vest. "Ken left it for me in the corridor. Your brother had some rather colorful words for me as well. I don't blame him."

"Don't start this again."

"I haven't done right by you."

"The letter, Patrick?"

"He says that he wrote to Anastasia ahead of this one for confirmation. I also have reason to believe he's coming to kill me. He should."

"I make my own choices, and I chose you."

"Marry me now and it'll be our secret. You can still have your other wedding and no one will be the wiser."

"Save the courts, which will publish it in the papers."

"So we'll go off. We'll catch a sub to Gretna Green and—"

"I shall be married once and it will be to you, before my family and yours," she added with a grin.

"I told myself I wouldn't touch you."

"But?"

His hands were in her hair and his lips on the back of her neck. That glorious tongue of his flickered down her jaw and lower until it found a home in the space between her breasts. The moistness that only he could bring reappeared with a burning need that threatened to consume. His wicked hands pulled up her dress and she struggled with the buttons of his vest and shirt.

"No." He redirected her hands to his trousers. The hardness there had her thighs quivering, and she found herself begging for him.

For this.

And soon he was inside her, spreading her open until she was sure he'd reached the deepest part of her. He didn't separate as he laid her down on the table, pushing aside everything to give her space. His wink served as notice that something was about to change.

Good lord.

He'd pulled her to the edge until her bottom was flush with him, then he hoisted both her legs into the air, one resting on each of his shoulders. When he moved, he hit new depths inside her and she bucked, unable to handle this onslaught of pleasure.

"Am I hurting you?"

"Yes. Don't stop."

She thought she heard him laugh, but she didn't have much of a mind left to spare for him. While he shoved in and out of her, he put one palm across the top of her nubbin, leaving his fingers resting on her curly hair below. But the hand wasn't just resting. It pushed, it rotated, it ground, it turned and propelled her to a new level of heaven. "Please?"

"Please what?"

"I don't know. Just...something...now."

And, waters bless him, the man answered her plea.

Chapter XIV

The four of them left under the watchful eye of Mrs. Huxton, though they pretended not to notice, and arrived at the Bane mansion under just as much scrutiny. For the last three intersections before his street, Patrick counted no fewer than six well-dressed men "lazying" about on corners. He knew a heavy fist when he saw one. What most annoyed him wasn't the spying on visitors but that alternative means of egress wouldn't be possible.

He leaned back and focused on the array of colors and lace around him. Both the women dazzled tonight, but Moira blazed with it. Even in this dark cycle-carriage, the blue of her dress shone like the morning in shallow waters. Her hair had been woven into a series of buns and dips atop her head, and he longed to set it free. Deep blue jewels hung around her neck, cascading to that joyous place between her fleshy orbs. Twice she caught him staring. Both times he'd smiled, shrugged and turned away.

Too soon, it was all business, and they were inside the gilded estate. He gave the attendant his name, but before the quartet was announced in the hall, they divided into two pairs. Only he and Moira used their true names. It was gamble, but *if* any of the women here had acquaintance with Kennerick, they weren't likely to explain the nature of it to their husbands. They'd arrived a little late. Late enough that the music was in full swing and their names largely unheard over it.

"Clock! Clock, my good man, over here!"

He waved to Bane and turned to give Ken the signal, but the man and his sister were already gone. "Ready, Moira?"

"Completely."

That was lie, and he knew it. Her lip quivered under the weight of it, and everything inside told him to kiss the worry away. And yet he couldn't. Instead, he had to force her right into the pit of fire. She kept up her brave front through introductions of the councilmen and their wives. The wee thing didn't even look back when the group split off and the women went to talk behind fans and animated hands.

"She's more lovely every time I see her, Clock. How did you win such a prize?"

He chose his answer with supreme care on the likelihood that they had done some investigating of their own. "Her brother and I are in the same trade. Old schoolmates as well. If I marry into the family, Old Man Gear is less competition and more of a, shall we say, expansion of my reach. Where there's new business, there's new opportunity for profit."

His remarks earned a slew of "quite rights" and "that's the way of it." The more reserved among them nodded their heads and whispered amongst themselves. However, at the back of the pack stood a nearly motionless man as tall as himself.

Mosten.

The man's wealth dripped off him in glittering fingers, a gold-topped walking stick and a nose that never seemed to leave the air. Mosten stared at him openly, smirking and nodding in something akin to approval when Patrick didn't avert his gaze.

The silver-haired man turned around to address someone else or perhaps just to give Patrick the brush-off, but it allowed Patrick a full view of the scene. He took a step back. A real one. Mosten was a shark. *The* shark. And all the rest of them – Banes, Eaton, Myles, the whole lot – were worthless remora fish, hanging around, desperate for his leftovers, sucking off his flesh, his profit, his power.

His mind worked overtime, trying to sort out what he knew of Mosten. Not much. He'd been a venture capitalist, pushing for private ownership of certain tunnels and the creation of for-profit hubs. He owned companies under and above water. But if there was anything tying him to the disappearance of young boys, he wouldn't be stupid enough to let it sit around, and that meant all hope rested upstairs with Kennerick, prowling through the belongings of the one among who *might* be dense enough to make a misstep.

His eyes wandered around the room, searching out Moira. She sat in the thick of it, inches separating her face from Mrs. Bane's puffer ink–stained teeth. Moira's beautiful features gave nothing away – if you didn't know her. Her locked and frozen face registered with him as surprise. She might fool them, but not him and not that anyone else was looking.

Every single woman in the gaggle – all of them – leaned in to hear Mrs. Banes. A few fanned her. A few more fanned themselves.

Moira turned around and caught him looking, then smiled at him.

Correction.

She smiled right past him. He whipped around to see the other side of the room, but no one was there. Before he could go back to where Moira *should* be, Bates came up to introduce him to another crony.

Every so often, he'd check back to ensure that Moira was still there.

And she was.

Until she wasn't.

He hadn't even lifted his foot to find her before some jackanapes put a hand to his shoulder and asked him about his latest case. It was the very last thing he had on his mind at the moment, but he caught a glance of Mosten eyeballing him and didn't dare risk giving Moira up. If she was in danger, she'd scream. And she hadn't been running away from something, but to it. For now, he had to trust that. The alternative of setting Mosten's interest on her wasn't an option.

And so he stood and listened to men talk about themselves.

Their money.

Their family names.

And most of them, save the nouveau riche, tried asking the same of him. They left him no choice other than to play along.

"Bane says that you're considering joining the brigade. Is this true?" Johns or James or hell, somebody asked. "Would Matron Clock have approved?"

Ahh, the question that hung round his shoulder like a damned iron cloak. How many of these families had been investigated by his? He'd never know and neither would they, though that was hardly the question. The issue was legacy, as it always was with these types.

He'd fallen prey to it, but not anymore. Not since Moira. "I know my place in this world. Matron put me on a good path, but it's up to me to make something of it. I'm confident about where I place my steps these days. I'm a man with my eye cleverly on the prize, sirs. I'll take what gets me there."

This mollified the crowd somewhat, and they split into smaller groups, each congratulating themselves on their latest profit margins.

Mosten took to the dance floor with his daughter...or wife; they were just about the same age. It gave Patrick time to excuse himself for privacy matters, and he went out the side door he'd seen Moira go through far too long ago.

It led to an empty, half-lit room with several sofas. "Empty" being the most important word. He took the door at the other end of it. This gave way to an even dimmer corridor, with five doors on either side.

"Moira? Moira!" It wasn't quite a shout, but well above a whisper. He pulled at his necktie, suddenly too tight, and wiped damp hands against his legs. "Moira? You'd better answer or I'll bring this whole thing down."

One door near the end of the hall opened and a man slunk out, leaving the door ajar behind him. Shadows hid his face, but he was tall and slim, yet careful to stay out of the light.

"Who are you?"

"She's there. She's fine. You'd better hurry, though," he said, pointing to the ceiling. "It's all about to come tumbling down."

Patrick's thighs pumped, taking him to the room where he imagined all sorts of atrocities.

None of which were as bad as what he actually saw: Moira, half naked, grinning from ear to ear and with a man's hands all over her body. He may have growled. He for damned sure saw red, and his fist curled as he picked up his pace towards the pair.

"Patrick!"

"Shut up."

"But Patrick, it's Hellion!"

"Shut...what? Get your hands off her." One thing stopped him from destroying them both. Hellion produced a small knife. And actually, it didn't stop him, just slowed him enough to reach for his own.

Moira huffed and rushed between them. "That's enough."

"How could you do this to me, Moira? Why?"

"Do what? Oh, you can't possibly think—"

"Be quiet. I don't want to hear—"

"You just asked me to tell you—"

"And now I'm telling you to shut your mouth or—"

"Or what? You'll shut it for me? You love me too much for that. I know you do, even if you haven't said it. And you know I love you too much for this. Look beyond your rage, silly boy. Look!"

He did.

Still half-naked.

But...covered in papers.

"She—"

"Quiet, Hellion. Moira, I need you to explain exactly what's happening, right the hell now."

She pointed to the papers, bound with strips of fabric. "Proof. Proof of everything we've been looking for. Names, numbers, dates."

"If I may?" Hellion waited for his nod to continue. "I was upstairs when I saw your brother or whatever he is. We were of the same mission, I presume. He found some papers and I found other papers and we grabbed until, well, the boy big came."

"Big boy?" Moira asked. "You didn't mention that."

"Rather busy."

"Talk me to me, not her, Hellion. And you, get the dress up. Or down. I assume there's a damned good explanation for this."

"The absolute best," Hellion said. "So, I grabbed my papers and started out, but all the exits are guarded and, well, I could hardly walk out with a stack of papers."

"Then you saw Moira and put your hands on her?"

"I didn't enjoy it."

"He didn't, Patrick. Really."

He didn't blame her. Well, now. That look of innocence and certainty couldn't be faked. At least not with him. Hellion, on the other hand, would be dead the next time they met.

In all his murder planning and body disposing, he'd missed one tiny little thing that Moira hadn't.

"Where's Kennerick now?" she asked.

"I reckon getting his face destroyed. I tried to tell you. We heard steps and ran. I may have shoved him in the hall with Big Boy to save myself. Then I ran downstairs to hide in here."

Any other questions would have to wait. A woman's blood-curdling scream from upstairs wasn't the least bit hampered by walls and floors. It had been timed perfectly, if one was sadistic enough to do that sort of thing. It happened just as one song ended and another was set to begin.

It didn't, of course.

That would require music. And music required sheets. And to read those sheets required light.

Those went moments after the scream.

The sequence of events would be hilarious over tea one day. One scream. Total darkness. Then dozens of screams, indicating the lights had gone out everywhere. A sliver of it shone through the window from the streets.

He looked at Hellion for a heartbeat and together they ran for it, shoving and grunting to get the damned pane up.

"Let me help," Moira cried out behind them.

"Man's work."

"You'll get in the way," Hellion added.

"But I can help. Damn you two men and move!" And there she was, heavy chair in front of her.

Hellion bowed and took one end. Patrick grabbed the other and together they smashed the ground window. Moira crawled out first, dress still not done up. Hellion followed and Patrick pulled up the rear.

Outside, Hellion didn't give him a chance to ask more questions, disappearing in the throng of running guests. Clock would deal with him later. For now, he took Moira's hand and they pushed their way to the corner of the street where Anastasia's cycle-carriage and driver waited.

He reached for the door but found himself yanked inside by a busted-lipped Kennerick and a black-eyed Anastasia. The second they were both in, the driver took off, pedaling them away from the confusion behind them.

Chapter XV

Anastasia rested her head in her brother's lap in the jostling carriage. "I'll go first."

"I need to hear from Moira first," Patrick said beside her.

Kennerick pinched his bleeding nose and held back his head. "No. Our story is really good. Can't believe I broke my nose again."

"Not now, Kennerick. My intended as something to say. Moira?"

"Patrick, nothing happened."

The other half of the carriage got suspiciously quiet, and she turned to see both siblings sitting straight up and elbowing one another. She finished doing up the front of her dress and told Patrick the truth. "Hellion came to get me."

"I saw that."

"But I couldn't go right away."

"I saw that."

"But when I found him, he wasn't alone."

"Who?"

"I don't know, another man. He helped Hellion—"

"Two men touched you?" Whether she could label Patrick's interjection a shout, howl, moan or general question, she wasn't sure.

Anastasia started humming and Kennerick whistled. One look from her and they both went silent.

"I should go back a step. When I saw him with another man, I mean that I saw him *with* another man. They were...uh...that is...the man was sitting on his lap. It was most evident that they were quite happy with one another."

This time, Anastasia whistled and Kennerick outright laughed and turned to Patrick. "So you walk in and see her with two men, only—"

She didn't know what stopped him from finishing that, her look or Anastasia's loud smack. It didn't matter. She needed to focus on Patrick, whose scowl dropped to more acceptable levels. "I see."

"That's it? No grand pronouncements. Am I free to live?"

"I didn't mean—"

"If you can't trust me, then why are we getting married?"

"What was I supposed to think with some man down your dress?"

"You weren't supposed to think anything. All you had to do was have faith in me. How hard was that?"

"What if you'd walked in and seen me with some woman?"

"My sister can make that happen," Kennerick added.

Patrick's head snapped up. "You say one more thing and I'll throw you out of this carriage."

Anastasia's two-fingered whistle shut everyone up. "It's my carriage and no one will be doing anything other than calming the hell down. Let's all take a nice, deep breath and consider what we've accomplished. I assume this brouhaha concerns the papers Moira's sweating over? Well, fine. We have them. I look like the street fighter on the wrong end of things, but we have our bloody papers. We're alive and we weren't caught."

"And the free drinks," Kennerick added lamely.

"There's that too."

"How did you two get out?" Patrick asked. "That was you, with the lights, wasn't it?"

"That's what I tried to tell you two. I came around the corner to see my sweet baby brother getting a fist to the face. I won't have that. I'll never let anyone hurt my angel."

"She loves me."

"I do. I couldn't stand by while this happened and I grabbed a vase, came up behind the man and smashed it over his head."

"And he fell," Patrick finished for her. "Well done."

"He didn't fall. Why does everyone in this carriage refuse to let people finish talking? As I was saying, for the third time, I hit him over the head, which had no effect. The man's built like a whale. He turned, which gave Kenny the opportunity to stab him with one of the broken shards."

"And that dropped him," Moira added.

"No, and you two are perfect for one another. Fourth time and I will finish, if you please. So the whale does not drop. So I grab another shard and slash him across his private parts. No interruption needed, Patrick, I'm nearly done. Then Kenny punched him and I punched him and kicked him, though in the end, I think the blood loss did it."

"Is he dead?"

Anastasia rolled her blue eyes in her direction. "No. Now, I'm finished. Anything else we'll talk about in the morning. This thing with your neighbor – we need to get Moira in the house unseen. Take my carriage and—"

"I don't care anymore, Huxton can be one of the witnesses to the wedding. Kennerick, tomorrow I need a priest."

"What?" three voices asked in unison.

"A priest, if you still want me, Moira."

Things had long changed since they'd first made their agreement. She'd wanted a proper wedding back then, perhaps because she hadn't anticipated a proper marriage. Things were well different now. It wasn't the wedding that mattered anymore. Just the man. And she'd take him any which way she could. "There's but one way to properly answer that. I do."

Kennerick snorted. "Disgusting."

Anastasia yipped.

And Patrick, sweet Patrick, brought her hands to his lips. "I do too."

Chapter XVI

She'd slept like a log that night, wrapped in his arms. They didn't make love – no energy – but it didn't mean the absence of it. No, love came to her in the quiet times like this, gently. That was almost as good. She woke up splayed across his chest and intended to wake up the same way and for the rest of her life.

"What are you smiling about, woman?"

"Us."

"Is that an invitation?" He flipped over until he trapped her beneath him. "Shall we work on our family now? The next generation awaits," he said. His morning ruff tickled her chin in the most delightful way.

Her future lay next to her and yet, she couldn't fully see around the cases to get there. She'd mulled over a single thought the whole night. Not about the wedding, but a child. "I know why Bane went along with it. I even understand it a little. I don't forgive it, or condone it, but...well..."

"Not an invitation." Patrick flounced back onto the bed but laced his fingers through hers. "What's wrong? Is it my life? It's dangerous, but I'll protect you. I'll take on financial cases instead and—"

"That would kill you and I wouldn't ask it. This isn't about that. It concerns a child. One specifically. Mrs. Bane had a daughter."

"No she doesn't. Bane only has boys. What has that do with anything?"

"Had, Patrick. One she loved with the whole of her heart. Then one day, about five years ago, she took her out for a walk. She'd gotten tired and fussy, so Mrs. Bane held her in her arms instead of using the pram. Some tunnel children approached her, begging for food and money. She tried to shoo them away, but the baby fell when they rushed her. The tiny head didn't survive the fall."

"It doesn't excuse what Bane is doing. But..." His voice faded off and he fluffed his pillow. "It's been weighing on you, hasn't it? Are you certain you want this life?"

"It'll get easier. I want you. And adventure."

"They'll be plenty of that, Mrs. Clock."

"Mrs. Clock. Mrs. Patrick Clock. It sounds good."

"Rolls off the tongue."

Interesting phrase. It reminded her of something Anastasia spoke of during their tutoring session. She dipped beneath the blanket, pushing all thoughts of anything but Patrick away. She grinning as his body stiffened against hers.

"What are you doing?"

She didn't answer. Her hands dragged down his body, thumbing his nipples as her fingers passed by. Dare she? Why not? Hadn't Anastasia said that this was the thing that shocked, destroyed and resurrected men?

She had a mind to find out, and as he bucked, grunted whilst inside her mouth as he screamed above her, she had to acknowledge that Anastasia had never once lied about a single thing.

Still slack jawed from the morning, Patrick went to the laboratory while Moira and Anastasia prepared for the impromptu wedding. There wasn't anything he could do at this point. A judge had been found and handsomely paid to circumvent decorum. Catherine was out gathering things for a large dinner and Moira...oh Moira.

"You're thinking about her again."

"I love her, Ken."

"Are you sure? Quite sure? It could be lust."

"It's not that."

Ken snorted and brought over another stack of dailies. "What I heard this morning says otherwise. What the hell did she do to you?"

"A step too far."

"Right. Well, I'll be staying with Anastasia."

"I appreciate it. Just a week alone—"

"I mean permanently."

"What?" They'd been together for so long that he hadn't considered living in this house without him. When he'd gone away to school, he'd done so with the comfort of knowing that Matron Clock was still protected by one of her boys. They'd grown up here, together. "This home is as much yours as mine."

"Agreed, and for now, I'll keep my office in attic. But I don't need to hear you two enjoying each other."

So he'd move in with a prostitute? But he kept his mouth shut, knowing that Anastasia wasn't a factory worker, so to speak. She managed from afar. It would be good for all of them – no one needed to live alone. "I'll miss my little brother."

"I'll be down the street. Really, you won't. I imagine you'll have other things to occupy your time."

"You'll miss me too."

"I will not," Ken said and then he hugged him. It was the oddest thing, but in all the years they'd been together, he'd never once been hugged by him. Be damned, he really would miss the bugger.

When Ken pulled away, his mind flashed back to the moment they first met. Two boys, one light, one dark, playing in the tunnels. It was Ken's growling stomach and an invitation for tarts that started their friendship. It'd been the truest one of his life. "I know you have your sister – real blood – but for me, I can truly say you were the only brother I ever had."

Kennerick smiled and leaned back down to the table full of old dailies. He opened one, paused and looked back over his shoulder. "Unless you know something about my mother that I don't, I can truly say the same thing. Hey, are you sure about this?"

"Not again, Ken."

"No, this," he said, pointing to the stacks of articles. "Researching some five-year-old accident on your wedding day. What does it matter?"

"Moira needs to know if it's true about Mrs. Bane. She needs some reason for this all to make sense."

"She's never heard of greed?"

"She's never seen it at play, I imagine. Marrying me will kill that innocence."

"I think you took care of that this morning."

"Stop it. Half of me thinks it'll be kinder to not show up."

"Because you're the bigger man?"

"I try to be."

"Is this the same bigger man who flew off the handle because a fully noninterested thief king touched her? Same man? You're not giving her up. You can't. Besides, I've hired a wagon to move my things already."

And there was his answer. Ken would club him over the head and chain him in a closet if he thought for one moment that this wedding was a mistake. It marked the highest approval. He responded to it in the only appropriate manner. He went to the other side of the massive table and started looking though another set of dailies.

Kennerick found it first. There, shining as bright as a pearl, were the words confirming the woman's story. Near four and a half years to the day, a small girl had fallen from her mother's arms after an attack by starved tunnel children.

Yet Mrs. Bane hadn't told Moira the whole tale. According to the article, the boys were summarily arrested, tried and brutally flushed out into the open water, all within two days of the incident.

"Will you tell her?"

"Can't, at least not the rest of it. It's her wedding day. Let her hold on to her happiness a little while longer."

"Glad we've got that settled."

"Because?"

Kennerick handed over a slip of paper. "It came in the post. No name. No sender. Just one word. *Run.*"

Non descript paper. Ink of average quality. Nothing spectacular about it at all. "How much to read into it that it arrived on my wedding day?"

"Nothing. No knew but you, me, her and the officiant. Hell, it could even be for me. I've slept with enough men's wives to warrant it."

"True enough." But there was nothing he could do about it. No real threat unless... His mind raced back to the first letter – the one in Grandmother's script. "You don't think it's the solicitor again? No, he's still away."

Ken rolled his eyes and crossed his arms. "Maybe it's possible. He's back in London."

"And you didn't bloody think to tell me?"

His brother grinned in that half-sheepish, half-congratulatory sort of way he did when he'd done something evil for the cause du jour. "I didn't tell you because it was a surprise. A gift. He's in the hospital. Broken ribs from a masked man with impeccable tastes in clothes." He popped his collar and straightened his tie. "I couldn't think of a better gift on such short notice."

Chapter XVII

"How in the waters did you manage to find a dress?"

Anastasia looked up with a smile splayed across her face but didn't stop sewing. "One of my girls got married. You don't mind wearing a prostitute's dress, do you?"

"Is she happy?"

"About to push out her third child. The little fool never stops grinning these days."

"Then I'm happy to wear it. It's good luck."

"Because it's not too late. We can leave now and you can come and stay with me."

Moira tweaked the nose of the teasing woman. "Do you think your brother is making the same offer to Patrick at this very moment?"

"No. That man will never find another woman like you. He knows it. We all do."

"And I'll never find another man like him."

"I suppose. Something's changed, Moira. Your feelings about this, I mean."

Maybe. When she'd done the bizarre thing of proposing to Patrick, it'd been for the material benefits of marrying like to like. And yet this was so much more than a business arrangement now.

Anastasia laced up the back of the too-large bridal gown and directed her to turn around.

"Now that I think I love him, I wish for more time. I want my mother here." She stepped away to pull forth a small fabric cache of treasure she kept on the top of her dresser. "See these? Fig seeds from home. Out in those waters, everyone has access to the surface – enough for planting some small subspecies of plants. My several-times-great-grandfather brought back a fig tree from his old home. We keep pruning it back, of course, but ever since then, it's been there. When one of us moves off, we take a few fruits and plant a new beginning. He made his sons promise that one day, when the waters went away, the seeds would be planted in the ground – actual ground – and the tree would reach its full height again. We plant and prune until that happens."

"That's why you brought it with you, isn't it? In case you never went back?"

"I always meant to return, but this was a small part of me rebelling, I suppose. I'm glad I did it now. Every woman in my family has the fruit or leaf of a fig in her hair on her wedding day. At least I have these."

"Such a strange place, your waters. Land and large trees. It's a wonder you even eat seafood."

"You'll love it. I'll take you there, assuming my family is still speaking to me after this."

"Don't be silly. It'll take a lot more than this to stop talking to you."

Moira took a much-needed hug from her new sister and one whose friendship she hoped to have forever. If worse came to worst, she'd weep over the loss of her old family, true, but she could do it on the shoulders of her new one. A weight she hadn't known she'd carried dissipated, replaced by the fullness of new love and new family in a husband, a sister and yes, even a new brother.

Anastasia had to swat her away. "Enough of these tears. We've work to do. Straighten your back. I'd hate to get blood on this fine white dress I labored so hard to find."

"Blood?"

"Stop twisting. I'm going to sew a few of these seeds into the lacing right here. When we give the dress back, we'll remove this little piece and we can sew it into your daughter's dress when the time comes."

"We?"

The clarification never came. Catherine rushed through the door, dress smudged, face covered with baking powder. "It's Mrs. Huxton, ma'am. Says it 'portant. Duties as a guest and such. I don't mean to bother ma'am, but she's in a fair tizzy."

"I'll go." Anastasia started to rise, but Catherine shook her head.

"She says she'll only speak to Himself or the lady, and I don't think mister is in a state of dress so ta speak."

"You're married with a full passenger list of children, but you can't knock through the door of a half-dressed man?" Anastasia asked, hands on her hips.

Moira stepped between them with a hand on both of their shoulders. She nodded from one woman to the other before walking from the room.

The older woman met her at the bottom of the stairs, pacing and wringing her hands. Moira pasted on her best smile and tried to speed this along. "Mrs. Huxton, I'm sorry that we haven't been properly introduced."

"Nothing about this has been proper. You skulking about, wearing men's clothes and – don't look at me as if I'm stupid. I'm old, not idiotic. You've been living in sin and it's about time you did the right thing. Carrying on like that. You may have fooled the rest of these halfwits, but not me."

"Mrs. Huxton, I...that is..."

Then the woman winked and leaned in. "I wasn't always a widow, girl. Or old. Everyone needs a good sin or two, but that's neither here nor there."

"But—"

"There's someone about the house. Dark-skinned, like you. Well dressed. Young. He's been walking past this house the whole morning, looking and pretending not to. I know Clock's business – even helped out the old Matron back when we were as fast and loose as you—"

"Mrs. Huxton!"

"This man's up to no good. I can smell it. I do mean that literally. His pipe wafted all over. It ought to be criminal."

"Pipe? Did it carry the aroma of cinnamon?"

"Don't know that I'd say aroma."

"Papa!" She'd bother with excusing herself when she got back. For now, her feet scuttled her away, taking her to her father's arms. It was ridiculous to think he'd have received the most recent letter, but maybe he'd stumbled across the first one. She didn't delude herself into thinking he'd come with a smile on his face, but she was still his daughter and it was enough that he'd come at all. Maybe she couldn't make him understand from afar, but with him here, there was that chance.

Or not.

Her father wasn't here. Instead, the hands on her shoulders that wrenched her around with such force that she yowled in pain belonged to someone just as close and just as angry. Her screech didn't lessen the skin-digging grip, but it managed to do a few things.

It stopped two bikers so fast that one crashed into the other.

It had Anastasia screaming out the now-open top window.

Mrs. Huxton started beating her attacker with her cane.

And it had Patrick rushing out the door, knife raised in his hand, face set on murder. That wouldn't do. He had enough to overcome with her father without adding the murder of her brother to the list. "Patrick, wait."

He didn't.

Then again, neither did Michael. Apparently, hearing Patrick's name snapped something within him. His eyes narrowed, his fists curled and his lips pulled back in a half growl that sent her thudding heart into a panicked beat. "Michael, stop!"

If Patrick recognized her brother, he sure didn't act like it. He did nothing other than launch, shoving his blade in Michael's direction. Her brother twisted, but not fast enough to avoid a bloody gash across his arm. This sent Mrs. Huxton into a dead faint...if one could qualify a slow descent to the ground with one eye closed and the other firmly locked on the action as a dead faint.

"You bastard. She's my sister."

"You touch my wife again and—"

"Wife?"

It took her pushing and Kennerick's pulling to separate the two fools. Michael swiped the back of his hand across his bleeding mouth. "Get your things. We're going home."

"I am home."

Then he looked at her. Really, looked. "Why are you wearing that?"

"Why do you think?"

Michael's neck jerked back to a somewhat restrained Patrick. "Why the rush? What did you do?"

Patrick's grin was positively lecherous. "Everything she asked me to."

That set off another round of swears and skin-splitting punches, half of which missed her, Kennerick and the recent combatant, Anastasia, who took swings at the both of them.

"Enough. Enough," Anastasia said, in a voice as cutting as the blows. The thin but fierce woman glared from man to man, an accusatory finger in each chest. "You're the ornery brother?"

"Ornery?"

Anastasia waved his question away. "They're getting married because they love each other and because they're well suited. Never mind the gift that's eight months away."

"Eight? She's only been gone a month at best!"

"He's a handsome man and they've known each other for much longer than you realize. She's been working this case for two months with him by correspondence. When she came down here to stay with me, they fell madly in love. Who are you to stand in the way of that?"

"Her brother!"

"Think about that before a wee thing comes along to call you 'uncle.' Do you want him knowing that you tried to keep his mother from becoming an honest woman?"

"You're lying. I know my sister and—"

"She's not." The resurrected Mrs. Huxton, now on her feet, inserted herself in to the midst of the foray. "The man came to me in almost tears after their tryst. He wanted to marry her ages ago, but she kept waiting for her family's approval. She seduced him."

Patrick threw his arms in the air. "This is ridiculous. She didn't—"

"Nothing to be ashamed of," Kennerick said. "At least it's in the open."

"I'm afraid it was my idea. I told her that my former husband, rest his soul, hadn't been able to resist a certain thing," added Anastasia. "I may have planted a seed."

"As did I," added the red-faced Mrs. Huxton. She shrugged off their looks. "I'm old. Not dead. She wanted a man who would appreciate her mental talents as well, Mr. Gear. She's a good girl. Smart and going about this business of helping strangers. She needs a man who will let her carry on. That's Clock. He's a fine lad. Come from a good family. Why, his grandmother fair sent a note from the grave to bless this."

She had no idea what the woman went on about, but Patrick's jaw dropped. Kennerick tried to excuse himself, blabbering about a solicitor or something, but Mrs. Huxton latched onto his arm.

"The Clock family is treating her better than yours is at the moment. This pirate-looking one right here is a doctor. He'll tend to your arm. Ahh, bless. Here comes the priest."

Michael rolled his eyes, but Anastasia hooked her hand through his good arm and led him towards the house. "I'll put the kettle on. Shut up and follow me."

Patrick, however, hadn't moved. "Mrs. Huxton?"

"Yes, Mr. Clock?"

Patrick and Kennerick looked like children lost in the wild and guilty sin between here and the end of creation. None of this made any sense at all, especially not the widow's smirking response.

"She trusted me to know when to send it."

Chapter XVIII

The wedding took no more than ten minutes. For all the rushing and fussing, fighting and cussing, the judge entered, said a few words, and with their signatures, they were husband and wife. In and of itself? Short and unfulfilling.

But on the grander scale of things, she'd won. She had him and Kennerick and Anna and even Mrs. Huxton. She had a new life and could find more than enough happiness in that.

Her brother and her husband...

She smiled and repeated the word over and over. *Husband. Husband.* It would take some getting used to. But no, her brother and husband still hadn't spoken since their pugilistic reintroduction before the wedding. Even now at what ought to be an exhilarating dinner, dark looks fired from one end of the table to the other.

The mood was so discomforting that even Mrs. Huxton had left, complaining of swollen ankles brought on by cinnamon smoke. The other set of siblings tried for small talk, but it fell flat and too forced to make any headway. That left one thing to do: retreat to the safety of murder.

A part of her hated that it would come to this – a discussion of the like on her wedding day – but then she realized that this *was* what she wanted. This was what made her family what it was. More to the point, there was no one thing that both men could sink their teeth into better than a good case. "Michael, can you trust a thief?"

"Is that what we're calling your husband?"

"You're not going to insult me at my table and in my house. You can get the hell out right—"

She cut Patrick *and* Michael off with palms out in both directions. "No, no. I meant, how would you handle a situation where the authorities stand on the wrong side of the law and the lone person who believed you was a known thief?"

"Is this the case?" He grunted at her nod and shoved some steaming mussels across the plate, swirling the green sauce into circles. "How high up does the corruption go?"

"To the top. City Hall," Patrick spat out. The fool laid his hand over hers when Michael glanced in his direction. She gave him a kick under the table, but he didn't go. "It would be good to know if this is happening outside of London. If it's a municipal thing, fine, we'll go above them. If it's larger than that...well, let's leave it at a thought I'd rather not entertain."

Michael fingers rapped against the table.

He lifted his glass without drinking.

He sighed and nodded and did everything other than ask for what he wanted. Waters save her from stupid men. "So here's the whole story..."

She told him everything she knew, with additions by Patrick and Kennerick as necessary. Soon he was leaning forward, putting up theories and bringing his own view of things. It wasn't anything they hadn't discussed a dozen times before, but it served as confirmation that they were on the right track. Then it happened. While Kennerick went to get the stolen paperwork, Michael apologized.

Somewhat.

"I can't believe I didn't think to use your talent for my business. Now I've lost a sister as well as an assistant."

"You've gained a brother," she added.

"I lost a sister. So what shall I tell Father?"

"That his daughter's loved and cared for," Patrick said over the rim of his glass. He threw back a drink and looked dead on at her brother, daring him to say anything different. Kennerick came back before he could, thank goodness, and laid a pile of documents next to Michael's plate.

He picked up the first off the stack, head shaking the whole time. "A contract for racehorses? Horses? In London? Who uses those? They're an unnecessary extravagance for piss-sure island owners."

"Note the ages, brother. Who needs horses ten and twelve years old? They're ancient at seven. And at these numbers? But if you replace the word horse with boy... See, Michael? No one notices one or two, but if we can show the scale of it, we can bring it down. We got the proof. We just need the boys."

"This is happening now? Right now under our noses? Listen, I'm catching the next submarine home. Moira, we're not done speaking about this," he said, waving his hand around the room. "As for you, Patrick, if you hurt her, I'll kill you. Expect a note from me in a week or two about the investigation."

Chapter XIX

They had a honeymoon of sorts.

After one full night in each other's arms, making love and learning how to please one another, they spent the next week in bed with sheets, maps and contracts splayed out between them. It wasn't how he wanted to spend his days, but at least she was there. In a sick way, he loved the mystery. If this hadn't happened, and if she hadn't been so stubborn, he'd have never met her.

It didn't make any bit of the crime less horrid, but together they could fix it and save lives. There was just the small matter of proof. These contacts wouldn't do it. They needed to find the boys, and it meant that instead of enjoying hours *in* her, he had hours next to her, reviewing all the mapped-out areas of London and surrounding areas.

Moira looked up from a chart and thumbed her reddened eyes. She hadn't been crying, but she'd spent all day like this, hunched over small script. "On the day I came to London, I met a girl on the sub. She said she'd heard rumors of deeper tunnels."

"Unlikely. Nothing below the sea floor."

"True, and that's what I told her, but what if we went up a bit? And what if it wasn't a proper tunnel? Maybe someone has a submarine parked in uncharted waters. Saying it out loud makes it sound rather silly, hmm?"

"You're trying. It's anyone's guess, but maintaining a sub that long wouldn't make sense."

"You're right. He wouldn't go down before going up. It would unnecessarily extend the depressurization process. That again brings us back to a slow business of going up."

"I'll have a visit with descent chamber manufacturers."

"We don't have time for that."

"What's the alternative? I suppose we could look for more evidence in desks and drawers, but how? We need an excuse to get back into one of their houses."

"They'll be prepared for it this time. We'll...we'll review these contracts again. There must be something here that we've missed. If they spoke in code about horses, there may be more code elsewhere," she said and leaned against his shoulder. "Perhaps this is not what I imagined."

He didn't dare ask for more. Whether she meant marriage or life as an investigator didn't matter. There'd be no going back. Letting her go was not an option. "Perhaps you'll have fewer regrets when—"

"Who said anything about regret? This is different, and I wanted different."

"Are you saying that for me or for yourself?"

"I'm saying it because it's the truth. Don't be morose. I married you. Doesn't that make you the luckiest man in the oceans?"

"Fair point."

"And that luck will continue. We'll start with what we know."

"We'll start with Hellion. We didn't exactly have time to talk when we last met. I half expected him to have contacted us by now. He may have seen something we missed. The problem will be in finding the bastard."

Moira clicked her tongue and slid out the bed to stand by the window. "That man has an army of boys. We find one, we find Hellion."

He didn't join her just yet, enjoying watching her piddle around and scrounge for clothes. He could help, or he could watch. Both were good options. She still wore trousers, but now without the stays and bindings, showing her full swells and curves.

"Are you going to stare or get dressed?"

"Both."

"Care to help?"

"If I do, we'll never leave." He should have done anything other than get up and brush his lips across her neck or turn her around to enjoy that pouty little mouth of hers. It meant a delay, but so what? He took her rough and urgent against the wall. He needed her closing in around him, giving him shelter and a measure of peace before going out in the world. She deserved better than this, but the selfish part of him took her without patience or preamble.

Moira met him halfway, clawing and grabbing, mewing beneath him, biting and kissing his chest in alternate turns. By some miracle not of his doing, she finished with him, and together they collapsed onto the floor.

"Moira, I'm—"

"That was unexpected."

"I know and...that is..."

"Good. That's the word you're looking for."

And it was.

Finding one of Hellion's boys required no great performance complete with a flashy watch and blank stares in the park. When a small thief reached for the dangling chain, Moira latched onto his arm with both of hers. Her husband whirled around and grabbed the boy's jerking shoulders.

The squealing child jerked and twisted but didn't manage to get free and wouldn't, not until she and Patrick delivered their message. "Tell Hellion—"

"I don't know who ya talkin' about."

Patrick picked up the boy by his soiled collar. His little feet kicked the air and his freckled nose scrunched.

"Do you want any more of your friends to disappear? Do you? Tell Hellion that we need his help to end this. Find him. Stop for no one. Steal nothing else. Here." He handed the lad a few pieces of coin. "That's for your trouble. Tell him to come to me tonight. Clock. That's all you need to say."

Back on his own two feet, the boy eyed him with open wariness, but the rascal took the coin just the same. "He won't come, but if'n he do and you hurt 'em, we'll all kill ya," he said before taking off in a run.

"You think he'll show?" Moira asked.

He shrugged, though the answer turned out to be a most certain "yes."

Hellion greeted them on their own steps, under the watchful gaze of Mrs. Huxton. Having made eye contact with the master of the house, the curtains fluttered, obscuring her face.

"That was fast."

"I teach my boys well, Clock. And, Mrs. Clock. I hear congratulations are in order. Word travels quickly."

"I see."

"I wasn't spying, Clock, if that's what that sneer is for. Not that it was in the dailies, either. Perhaps I missed it along with my invitation? We run in closer circles than you might imagine."

"Inside. We're not doing this on the street."

"No time. I'm a busy man and my boys have been *just* as busy. I'd appreciate it kindly if you didn't damn near choke them every time you met one. Which makes this conversation that much more annoying." Hellion produced a silver toothpick and scraped at his teeth. "Word on the street is that you're under investigation."

"Investigation for what?"

"Don't know exactly. Prior to that, I heard they were considering you to join them."

"Where are you getting this from?" Not that it wasn't true, but he'd be damned if people went about talking of his private affairs...especially to the likes of Hellion. "What bloody connection do you have?"

"My boys, Clock. I've got two enrolled in that training program."

"The boy in the police station that Patrick told me about?"

Hellion's grin shifted from suspect to conspiratorial. "Seems Mr. Mosten doesn't trust you or your husband. A raid is coming, but soon and how. Today? Tomorrow? You're on borrowed time."

"And you're just telling me now?"

"I sent a note."

"No you didn't."

Hellion's hand flew to his mouth. "How dare you question my integrity? I sent you a note. I told you to run."

"How was I supposed to know it was from you? Do you jump when anonymous people tell you to run?"

"Generally."

Moira, who'd still had her hand latched through Patrick's, shook her way free and started for the steps. "I'll get you the contracts. You hide them and—"

"No!" Though who said it louder, himself or Hellion, Patrick couldn't be sure.

"Despite your husband's vote of confidence, I'm on the move until this thing gets settled. Find a place and hide those papers now." Then Hellion tugged at the cuffs of his green suit and turned away.

Patrick grabbed his arm and yanked. "Wait. I need one of your boys to find Kennerick. His sister is Ms. Anastasia down the road."

"You're going to want to get your hands off me. Thank you. Now, a few of them have sisters who work for her. I'll get your Kennerick here," was the last thing the Thief King said.

Patrick met Moira in the doorway, still shocked at the speed with which information moved in the tunnels. Moira, however, had her eyes fixed on Mrs. Huxton's window. "What are you looking at?"

"Nothing, husband. Suggestions on where to hide everything?"

"A box at the bank or maybe at Anastasia's," he said, but she still looked right past him...

Right out the door...

And across the street.

Of course. Who would suspect the older neighbor of holding and tampering with evidence? Not a damned soul. "We'd be able to keep an eye on it the whole time. You're good."

Moira crossed her arms and winked. "I know."

"How can we be sure she is, though?"

"We can't, but I can sneak papers into her house the same way I snuck those contracts out of the dance. She wouldn't be the wiser. I'll just excuse myself and drop them off somewhere between the drawing room and the necessary."

They spent the next hour deciding which papers were to be transferred. Kennerick came over to help, and together they divided information on the case into thirds: necessary, perhaps and bait.

The latter was strewn about the drawing room and in Kennerick's lab. The former would go to Huxton and the rest would be sent to Anastasia's. Papers flew about them with every movement, and in the mix, some of Moira's drawings came loose. The one of Hellion landed on top. Patrick's thumb, oft licked to turn pages, smudged a bit of the graphite near the man's name.

Only it wasn't his name. It was the name Bane had given him, the one Hellion swore wasn't his: Tim Hilkreel. "Have either of you ever heard of any Hilkreels, aside from this one?"

Moira shook her head and went back to work. Kennerick didn't bother looking up, just waved him off.

The name meant nothing...until the anagram puzzler in his mind squinted and brushed the fog away. "Tim Hilkreel." The letters moved, swirling in his mind like dancers across a ballroom floor. "Tim Hilkreel."

"If you say it a third time, it won't change," Moira said.

But it did. "My God."

"What is it, Patrick?

"Tim Hilkreel is an anagram for *I'm the killer*."

Silence.

Then madness as both rushed to his side, peering over the table. Kennerick snatched a graphite from the pile and started charting out the letters, crossing them out as he spelled the words. "Bane was the killer. Where's the liquor?"

"Is the killer," Moira corrected. "I'll have taste of that."

Patrick ripped Kennerick's examination apron over the man's head and threw it to Moira. "Put this on under your dress. We're putting the contracts in its pockets and you're walking to Huxton's now. We'll handle the rest later."

They shuttled her off and kept working, but not more than an hour or two had passed before the thudding knock of the authorities threatened to sever the door from the hinges. Kennerick rushed to his attic to prepare for his part in this grand performance. Patrick sealed off the room below the stairs, prayed it remained hidden and opened the door.

He feigned shock and surprise, though very real anger boiled his blood and he twice had to loosen his collar.

"Mr. Clock, we have reason to suspect you in—"

"Bane, what is this about?"

Bane managed to look apologetic and every bit the bumbling fool he'd always thought the man to be. Perhaps that was the true genius of him...or the wickedness. "I thought we had an arrangement?"

Bane sucked his teeth and waved the group of eight officers by. "Check everything," he said before turning back to him "Dirty business, Clock, is what it is. I'd love to bring you on, but Mosten brought up charges of theft, you see."

"Theft! You know me better than that." And this crime was a lot less than the murders and kidnappings Bane had been party to.

"One of his guards said they saw Hellion crab-crawling out of a window. Then you and your missus. I told him they must be mistaken, but he is the head of the council."

"But you're the—"

"I have a duty to protect all, Clock. What would they say if I didn't look into this, just because you're a close and personal friend? I do have a reputation to uphold."

Mrs. Huxton peered over the rim of her teacup. "I have a right to know if they're coming over here next."

Her plan had gone wrong from the beginning, and she still sat with papers trundled around her waist. The sparsely decorated house left no place for her to hide a sum of documents, at least not between here and the toilet. And about the time she'd gotten desperate enough to ask, Huxton screamed, alerting her to the scene across the street.

In a sick way, she was appreciative of the woman's predilection for spying. From her first-class seating, the two of them had a clear view of the goings on at the Clock property. She dropped her hand to finger the strange fabric surrounding the woman's windows. What looked like white curtains from home were curiously threaded sheaths that allowed one to look out and not in.

Old Huxton sipped her tea. "You're impressed. You should be. The thread is spaced out, but the white picks up the light from the lamps—"

"Creating an optical illusion."

"Of sorts. A woman of my advanced age needs to be careful of her surroundings."

"Without question." And with a setup like this, the woman probably hadn't missed anything in the past fifty years. "How many secrets do you know on this street?"

The Widow Huxton tapped one yellowed, cracked nail against her mouth. "All of them. You're not the first to dress as a boy, my dear. Now, what's this about?"

"I can't say, not yet. We're working for what's good, but it seems our foe is bigger than we thought."

"So be better."

"It's not that simple, Mrs. Huxton."

"It is. Be smarter than they are."

She thought they had been up until now. She got up to pace, but Huxton yanked her back down again.

"Movement gives the illusion away, girl. Sit. Watch. Learn."

They sat for an eternity, well until after the lights of the tunnel dimmed for the night. When the policemen cleared the street, she got up to leave, but one more, Huxton stopped her. She leaned over and pointed. Sure enough, two officers stood with crossed arms on opposite ends of the street. "Follow me."

She had benefit of words when Huxton led her to the back of the house. Even a few gutturals, "*ohs*" and "*unbelievables*" as the woman led her to a secret hatchway. But all words and air left her entirely when the woman opened it, bringing her into full view of the sewer pipeline below.

"One word of this and they'll shuttle us both. Now, follow this pipe until you see another door. Take the stairs on the other side. It'll put you out right where you need to be."

"How...illegal. So illegal. And dangerous!" The thought of fumbling in the pipes and indeed the very foundation that kept them all safe and alive had her swallowing her heart back down into her chest. Huxton wasn't having any of that.

"Pish pish! Bad pipes lain and abandoned. The Clocks have known about it for generations and made good use of it."

"But you're not a Clock."

"More one than you, missy. Grisba told me about it many years ago, when we were both very young. This wasn't my husband's house, you know, it was mine. I grew up here and refused to leave."

"But the passageway?"

"Yes, yes. I've used it many times to be where I've most wanted to be. I assume Patrick knows about it, but perhaps not – he's never used it before. Now, go and take whatever's rustling under your skirts with you."

It was impossible. Amazingly impossible and yet here she was, traveling in the warren on the very damn seabed upon which they lived. Her excitement didn't last in the darkness.

The faint light from Mrs. Huxton's room collapsed to a small pinprick and grew smaller with every forward movement. She crawled on hands and knees and until her palms burned and she was certain she'd worn holes where her knees were.

But the pain was a welcome respite from the lung-collapsing, throat-clenching gloom that threatened to swallow her whole. Her ears popped and her fingers tingled. The darkness was too much.

Her hand scraped against something less smooth than everything else. The door? She balled her fist and punched up, but the thing gave way with ease. Her hands searched for her next move, and she climbed bit by bit up metallic rungs until she found another door.

It opened to yet another one a few feet away.

Immediately behind it, less than a hand's length away, stood a fifth door! Her hands went in search for a handle that she couldn't find. If there was a time to scream, this was it. With everything she had and for as long as she could, she cried out for Patrick.

The floorboards trembled as he ran, calling out her name. Ever the dutiful husband, he came. "I'm here. I'm here."

Warm arms lifted her from her feet as she fought back tears now too embarrassing to shed.

"How did you—"

"Long story."

"Talk fast." He placed her gingerly on the bed. Wide thumbs rubbed over the raised and bruising flesh of her wrists and he kissed the now darkening skin there. "What the hell?"

"The secret passage? I climbed through it."

"The what?"

"The...the thing under your house. Your grandmother didn't tell you? Mrs. Huxton said Grisba told her about it when they were young. She said it took her to...oh."

Oh indeed.

"To?"

"Right. Uh, how much did you know about your grandmother, exactly?"

Patrick shook his head, clearly not understanding what she wasn't sure she should give voice to. Whatever secret the women had, Mrs. Huxton had just revealed it to get her home safely and at great risk. "She's not nosey."

"She is."

"Well, Patrick, she is, but she has a good reason. She and your grandmother were close, I think."

"They used to be."

"Perhaps more than any of us realized. She believes she needs to look after you as a favor to Matron Clock."

Patrick snorted and heaved off the bed. "May I clarify the finer points for expediency? There's a secret tunnel that leads across the street?"

"Correct."

"How far out does it extend in either direction?"

"Not sure. You'll have to ask Mrs. Huxton."

"And she'll know because..."

"Your grandmother trusted her."

"That's a lot of trust."

"I'm fairly sure she earned it," she added under her breath, but didn't repeat it at Patrick's deep-throated "huh" from above.

"We'll deal with this later. I'm just glad to have you back. Follow me. Ken's bleeding down the hall."

Chapter XX

Patrick held down his struggling brother while Moira sewed another stitch in the skin above his shoulder. Sweat sluiced down Kennerick's strained face, but he bit into the wadded cloth and took the pain without benefit of liquor. No choice. He was both patient and medical instructor. Kennerick lasted long enough to tell her to drop boiling water over his flesh before passing out for the final time. With all wounds red, oozing, but closed, Moira stepped back and wiped her brow. "He's tough."

"He's musty."

"That too. How did this happen?"

"Bane's men threw his stuff around. That was all fine and good until one of them ripped a portrait of Grandma. He snapped."

"We'll get it fixed. We fix everything."

He wanted to make love to her. He wanted to have her right now, but Kennerick needed him here. Another view out the windows revealed that the watchers she'd mentioned were no longer visible. At least not from this vantage point. Across the street, the curtains fluttered and Mrs. Huxton looked back with her thumb in the air. "The hell? I think Huxton just gave me the all-clear sign."

"You can trust it."

Moira washed up in a small basin by the door, rotating her shoulders as she did. She sighed and melted under his palms as he tried to rub the weariness out of her.

"You should rest, love."

"I don't think any other woman can claim the week I've had. Though I wouldn't change a bit of it. Most of it."

"But some?"

"Just the bloody bits. Kennerick's finally gone to sleep. Walk me to bed," she whispered against his throat.

She had a look. *The* look. The one that had reduced him to begging once. "We're horrific nurses."

"Work fast."

He did, unbuttoning his pants in the hallway. They never made it back to the bedroom. The wall had to suffice and he had her against it, fighting with her skirts while her hands pulled him closer. Her ankles crossed behind his back and she shoved the whole of her perfect body down upon him.

They finished what they started on the threshold of their bedroom door. One hand grabbed her hips while he braced himself on the wall with the other. She finished first, thank God, but only just, and he followed moments later. It'd never be enough. He'd never be done with her.

He dropped her heaving body on the bed and held her close until her breathing evened out. With heavy feet, he slipped out of bed and down the hall into Ken's room. He kept the doors to both rooms open, ready to run to whoever needed him first. For now, he pulled his chair by the door, propped his feet on the stool and kept watch over the two people he loved most.

"I woke up alone."

He jerked awake, but Moira's words weren't meant for him. She sat on the edge of Kennerick's bed, dangling a meatpie over Ken's head. His brother reached, swung and missed three times before she laughingly relented and handing him the pastry.

"I never thought I'd see the day you two would not kill each other."

Ken bit into the food and his eyes rolled back. "That drawing hand of your wife's is good with sutures. She's a natural. And considering how often we get stabbed—"

"What?"

"He's having a go, Moira. Where did you get that food? You went outside?"

She twirled and nodded. "The officers are gone. I checked with Mrs. Huxton."

"How? Never mind."

Kennerick whistled for their attention. "There's paper in my pie," he said, waving a slip of something in the air. "Now that is truly spectacular."

Patrick grabbed it, read it and handed it over to Moira. "The children are being held at some warehouses," she said.

"It's almost certainly a setup."

Kennerick winced and nodded. "One that you will have to go to alone, as they know I have an injury. Though not one bad enough to keep me from my daily habit or keep you here. Well played, whomever," he said, hand raised in mock toast.

"I'm going with you, Patrick."

"I won't let you."

"But—"

"Moira!"

"This only works if we both go and before you try to talk me out of it—"

"I'm your husband!"

"And I'm still speaking. I'll remind you that I've seen the address. I'll find a way to get there one way or another. Either with you, where we can look after one another, or alone, where I'll be captured and face a slow and torturous death. Do you want that on your conscience?"

And there was his answer. She *would* find a way to escape – and he'd spend too much capital worrying about it.

"You two go. Catherine will be here soon. I'm fine. I'll do what I can from here."

"And what would that be?"

"Funny, Patrick. Haven't you learned by now? I'm a man of many talents. Go and keep our girl safe."

They left with daggers stuffed in every sleeve and boot. He added a miserciorde to the arsenal just in case, then wrapped a slip of metal around her. It was what he'd wear himself when going out into dangerous situations. It didn't fit well, her breasts must surely ache pressed against the metal, but she didn't once complain.

They took public transport to the large London hub, the place from which all the various main tunnels of London started and shot out into neighborhoods. It was also where one could hire private submarines. In and of itself, it was a beautiful, terrible and dangerous place. And he'd brought her to see the worst of it.

For the first time, he didn't lie and tell himself that he'd do better by her. He didn't dare think that things would be different in the future. This was their future, and to honest, he wouldn't have it any less dangerous and he wouldn't have it without her.

"Stop worrying, Patrick."

"I'm not. Honestly, I'm not. You're right with what you said yesterday. We are good. We're even better together. We solve this, save the day and move on to the next one."

"Agreed."

"Then that's that." He held fast her hand and together they walked toward the depot, where cargo subs below and boats above shipped goods throughout the world. It was a place that would have taken lifetimes to search without the warehouse number so conveniently placed in the meatpie.

His name was enough to get him past the gate. Whether that was due to his enemies or his own familial reputation, he didn't know and didn't question. They found the warehouse at the end of a set of tunnels, far removed from everything else with dim, residual lighting.

"This whole end of the complex and not a single soul. That's not strange, Patrick?"

"No more strange than us walking in past that customs agent back there."

"About that – aren't they meant to be wearing badges?"

"And there's that. Yes." He put his ear to the door but didn't hear a thing. "I'd tell you to stay behind me, but you'd go out of your way to do just the opposite."

"Patrick—"

"So I'll just say that the thought of losing you damn near destroys me. Don't you dare do anything to give that nightmare life. You understand?"

She answered with a kiss, then placed her hand on his, and together they opened the door.

They stepped into the room. The shock of immediately not finding children was violently overtaken at Moira's choked squeal.

He turned around and the blood in his veins crystallized at the grinning, scar-faced whale of a man with his arm around her neck. "Do one thing and I snap it."

"What do you want?"

"Move. Walk into that room right there. Good boy."

"I'm doing it, all right? Now let her go. Keep me."

"I'd like to keep her and make her scream real good, but the boss don't like his rules broken. Inside. Now."

The small circular door led to an empty room. He turned to face the man who held Moira and forced his muscles to relax. If the goon let her go to close off the entry behind him, there would be a brief second of opportunity.

He didn't.

Not really.

Patrick kept his eyes locked on the bastard, even as he was ordered to the rear wall. "This'll be your new home until the boss man gets here. Make yo'self comfortable."

Patrick walked backwards though, focusing on Moira, willing her to stay strong. Their nameless attacker did release her, but only to step away, kick Moira in the back and propel her straight into Patrick's arms. Less than a second later, the door slammed shut, cloaking them in darkness.

"Moira?"

"Before you ask, I'm fine. I'm also quite good at picking locks. It was one of the few things Michael taught me. Step aside." She turned against him and he caught the perfume of her hair powder.

"Am I to presume you have something in your hair?"

"A few pins, my love. I can feel it catching but...damn. It won't go."

He'd revel in the relief of having her neck still attached once they were out of this. For now, he worked with her to speed up that process. Everything around here was built on pressure and the controlling of it. Why not the lock too? He dropped to the floor and started crawling, his hands reaching out in all directions for a metallic box and the treasure he prayed to find inside. After traversing the length of the room, he tried kneeling, reaching higher and still coming up short.

Next, he tried standing and when that didn't work, restarted the process. It wasn't until his fifth crawl around that he found it, the emergency hand actuator. "Get your pins ready. On my word, turn. One...two...now, Moira! Right now!"

There were two audible clicks, a blast of air, and the dim light of the greater warehouse poured though. Freedom lay before them to the left...but what about the dark area to the right? A light panel was just visible. Moira beat him to it, but the instant she flipped it on, his stomach turned in on itself.

Chambers.

Dozens and dozens of chambers, filled with sleeping children.

Moira jutted pass him and pressed her face against the closest one. "Depressurization tubes. And look at the hooks on top. They were never in tubes to go up, that's why no one ever saw them. He drags them behind ships like cargo."

It was bad, and yet much worse. In such a state, they couldn't release the children – not without medical attention. It also meant that the whole lot of them, he and Moira included, couldn't make a running escape. Certainly wouldn't make it past Mosten's men, one of whom had already run off to spread the good news of their capture.

That's about when the pounding started. Heavy, angry pounding at the doors that shielded the children from view. He looked for a weapon, his wife already with her stiletto in hand. Both of them willing and ready to go down swinging. "I love you, Moira."

"No time for that now. Tell me tonight in bed."

"Damn sure, I will."

When the doors burst open, a legion poured in, and they found themselves completely outmatched. Mosten had come faster than he thought possible and with an army in tow.

A very small...

...mismatched...

...ragtag army...

...of children.

And leading it was gap-toothed thief.

"Hellion?"

"'Hello there, Clock and Clock. A certain doctor told me you and your wife went for a bit of an outing. If you don't mind, me and my boys thought we might stop by. Hope you don't take it as an intrusion." Then Hellion turned and his mask of bravado fell away. Hellion's face, always carefree or as blank as empty calcium parchment, reddened and twisted before he broke off into a wild scramble towards his encapsulated boys.

Patrick caught him midstride with an arm to the waist. Hellion shook him off, even as he tried to yell reason at the man. "You'll kill 'em if you open it, Hellion. Put it together. Think, you idiot."

As if turning off a light, the thin man cracked his neck, took a deep breath and brushed his lapels down. "Apologies. Go home, Clock, we'll handle it from here."

"Mosten will waltz in here at any minute with reinforcements."

"You don't think I came alone, do you? I have friends. The contracts – are they safe?"

He didn't share that he'd hidden them in the newly discovered secret tunnel beneath his home, but Hellion was content to accept his nod in answer. The King of Thieves caressed one of the tanks and blinked away what might be tears. "We have to get them to someone above Mosten. I don't know who that is."

Moira, who'd been stooped and talking to some of the wide-eyed children that'd come with Hellion, stood up. "I do. My brother has connections back home. We can get them printed in papers there, if not here."

"Me too."

Everyone not entombed in a stasis tank whipped around at the new voice. Its owner came with a crew of young men in their twenties or so. They all looked to Hellion and grinned. If Patrick had to guess, he'd put good money on these being some of the former members of Hellion's gang all grown up.

Moira, however, looked as though she'd seen a ghost. He followed her gaze to the leader of this new group. It took a while for the fog in his brain to dissipate, but he knew the face well. He'd seen it before, only aged a bit and suffering from palsy. "Is that..."

"Yes," Moira said. "How do you know?"

"Know? That's the man—"

"Precisely. That's the man I saw Hellion with that night. But how did you know? I thought you hadn't seen his face?"

"Th-th-that wasn't what I...really?" *Ahh shit.*

"Yes. Wasn't that what were you going to say, Patrick?"

"Not exactly."

The blond man pushed back a lock of hair and gave the most elegant bow he'd seen this side of royalty. "Mrs. Clock it is an honor to see you again. And Mr. Clock?"

"Yes? Samuel McCoy isn't it?"

"Quite right. A pleasure. You're good, you know. I've had a damnable time avoiding you," he said, toying with a gold and glittering livery collar around his neck.

"You and Hellion..."

"We met at a gathering of sorts sometime ago, but that's neither here nor there. My grandmère on my mother's side is owed a favor. I can make sure the contracts will get into the right hands and made public."

"I'll hold on to them, if you don't mind."

"I do. You see, Mr. Clock, I'll be the hero. Father will have no choice but to publically support me, despite my private matters, and I can reclaim my inheritance on my own terms."

Patrick extended his hand to the grinning Samuel. "Agreed, but with the condition that I collect the king's ransom McCoy offered me to find you."

"Done."

"Not quite," Moira said. She and Hellion stood next to each in similar stances of arms crossed and foot tapping. "We still have to get out of here."

Patrick looked over the group of boys, watching the smiles drop one by one. Some held hands of the younger ones, others chewed their lips and glanced about nervously. One in particular stood out, his mop of red hair shining bold in the light. "You. You're the boy working for Bane, aren't you?"

"Yessir."

"Go. Run now and tell him that you heard that his name is showing up in tomorrow's dailies. A couple of you men go with him and keep watch. Make sure he stays safe."

The small group ran off, but it wasn't enough. There were still too many here, much too young for this. "Hellion, take your boys and go."

"They're fighters. All of them."

"Not for this. If help comes, it won't be soon enough. Moira, you're going with them."

"I will not." She stood there, jaw set and hands on her hips – full of fire and life. He intended to keep her that away. "I won't be able to fight like I need to if I have to worry about you."

"I could say the same. We fight together, Patrick. No matter the threat."

Tears welled in her eyes.

His too.

And Hellion's voice cracked with them as he ordered the youngest of his boys out of harm's way.

Soon the room was quiet. The fifteen or so who remained gathered in small circles. Some sharpened daggers against the floor. Others cleaned their fingernails with them, but each and every person had a dagger in hand.

But when the fighting started, it hadn't come to them.

Dozens of young screams bounced through the corridors. The boys hadn't made it to safety. He grabbed hold of Moira's hand and ran with the rest of the men in the direction of the sickening howls.

Fighters where there. He didn't know if they belonged to Banes or Mosten directly. He only cared that he stopped them from hurting another child. He kept Moira at his back and rushed to the front of the melee.

Men in ripped cloths swung at the children but pulled back upon their approach. One grabbed a child and used him as a shield.

To hell with that.

Patrick jumped over the lad, knife in hand, and plunged it into the neck of the bastard who held him. Moira screamed behind him, but by the time he'd turned, she'd shoved her blade into another man's chest, with the help of a grinning Samuel McCoy.

"Pull back. Pull back!"

The cowards retreated, scrambling toward the exit. He didn't have the heart to cheer with Hellion's men. While Moira jumped and hugged, he watched. Waiting. Only Hellion seemed to notice. "What is it, Clock?"

"This isn't over. The chambers back there are still filled with children."

"Then take her home while you still can."

Moira chuckled so softly that he almost missed it. She didn't say anything, just took his hand and walked back the way they came, not stopping until she reached the encased boys. "We'll wait right here. Together."

Five minutes passed.

Maybe ten.

No one complained. In fact, the opposite. The thieving lot sang and laughed. Some introduced themselves. Others kept away. But they'd all fight again – he knew that as sure as he knew of his love for the woman beside him. "If we get out of this—"

"When we get out of this."

"Fine. I'm having Kennerick doctor up something to keep you sedated for times like this."

"You can try if you want, but you'll fail. Grandly. I go where you go."

Before he could correct her, screeching and shouting reverberated through the tunnels. Each of them braced themselves, men, boys and woman, to fight.

No one spoke. He kissed his wife once more and waited for the new threat to emerge.

The doors didn't so much open as shatter.

Moira squealed and clapped her hands as the meatpie maker's son rushed in ahead of a host of people. Some he recognized as daily sellers or street vendors, but most he couldn't place at all.

The pie maker's son had his hand latched around a slender, bejeweled hand. "Anastasia?"

The sister of his heart winked and shrugged, but it was the humble gap-toothed boy who spoke first. "They made my Pa bake it and watched until Missus went away wi'it. But Pa knew Doc's sis and made me run as soon as Missus left."

"You have many more friends than you know, Clock," Anastasia said. "More importantly, so do I. One of my girls has a client rather close to the crown. Kenny told me everything. I told her everything and sent her off."

"How close to the crown?"

"His mother wears it. Not to take anything away from my sweet baby brother. One of his lady friends is also rather close to the crown."

"Dare I ask how?"

"Her mother wears it."

"Oh, my beloved philanderers." Moira rushed to capture Anastasia and the young boy in her embrace. He squealed and laughed in her arms.

"Everyone knows, Missus. I waited. I waited until I saw the men runnin' ta Mosten. 'Cause I knew, I did. Pa told me to tell evry'one and I did. The whole city's gone mad. You did it, Mr. Clock. You stopped 'em right and proper!"

"I didn't do a damned thing. Not really. It was my wife. This is all the work of my wonderful wife."

Chapter XXI

Two months later

Moira squared her shoulders and walked into Patrick's study. Even surrounded by piles of papers and mountains of maps, he looked up and smiled. And why not? They were heroes, and new cases had come in with each day's post since they'd solved the case of the lost boys. They hadn't yet agreed to a single one. Lord McCoy had paid the finder's fee for his son, and they could sit comfortable off it for a few years or more. Never mind the inheritance now set free by their wedding. Still...

She held up two letters in her hand.

"New cases?" he asked.

She waved the one on scented paper. "This is from a lady who wants me to find her sister. Her father gave up the by-blow years ago and she feels a woman can best handle this. Me – not you! My first case. I'm not here to ask permission."

"Perish the thought."

"I'm taking the case, Patrick."

"Figured."

"Then there's this one. It's from my father."

That had him standing straight up. He plucked it from her hands and brought it to the light, snorting before he'd even finished opening it. His face transformed in rapid succession from pinched to relaxed to outright shock. "He's coming here."

"Yes."

"And bringing your mother."

"Yes."

"And wants to know where your brother is."

"Not precisely sure how to explain his and Anastasia's...friendship."

"Quite. The last two letters from him have been promising, but I still have my concerns."

"He wouldn't kill me in front of your mother, would he?"

"Doubtful. I consider this a good second step. And one more."

"You said two letters." He turned back to her father's note and waved it. "One. Two."

"Of sorts." What she handed him next wasn't a letter. Just a calendar...one with circled days and question marks and a tiny, hand-drawn cradle with their initials on the side.

"Are you?"

"I think so."

And then he was there, arms all around, lifting her and shouting, with a smile as wide as the moon. "Thank you, Moira."

"I didn't do it alone."

"Thank you for my life. Thank you for my dreams coming true."

"That's what I'm meant to say to you, silly man. I love you. I love this life and I already love the new life we've made."

"Then come upstairs with me, Lady Inspector, and let us make some more memories for you to love."

Thank you for reading. Keep turning to read the first chapter of Kennerick's story, The Doctor of London.

THE DOCTOR OF LONDON
Chapter One

Kennerick strongly considered kicking the bicycle from underneath the boy's scrawny legs. Unfortunately, there were too many witnesses. Jumping out of the way was just as easy.

He didn't hate children. Some, he went out of his way to almost like.

Kennerick bit into the meat pie and fought the urge to groan in delight. The kid who made this? That one, he liked. Never mind that the boy had saved his arse a time or two. His mood improving as his stomach filled, he strolled on.

During weekends, the tunnels of Water London hummed with activity. Ladies trotted from one shop to the next as the arms of their beleaguered maids sagged beneath baskets of wrapped goods.

Beneath the water's surface, the silvers and blues of his city were turning an annoying shade of pink. Ridiculous. Taxes were on the rise, and they couldn't think of anything better to do than dye the damned waters?

It was stupid. But then, stupid people were all over London.

"Merry Valentine's Day, sir. Card for the missus?"

"Out of my way." Kennerick shoved the vendor to the side and headed toward his townhome, still too many streets away.

Waning in and out of popularity, Valentine's Day was by far the most irritating date on the calendar. Only the very wealthy and very poor seemed to care about it anymore. And although he now had a good deal of money now and yes, had been born a beggar in the tunnels, he never fully counted himself among either group.

He didn't like groups anyway.

Kennerick identified himself very solidly as the sole member of the Clever and Honestly Unrepentant Physicians of London. More to the point, very few people in the city were worth speaking to, and three-fourths of them were gone – quite literally.

Kennerick turned away from the tunnels that so reminded him of his humble beginnings. Both his streetwise birth sister and his adopted brother were away on holiday with the loves of their lives. He'd declined the invitation to join them, opting for loneliness rather than hearing their *un*loneliness through too-thin walls.

Head bent, he shoved the remains of the meat pie in his mouth, clasped the lapels of his jacket together and soldiered through the crowd. The lighting and heating functions in the massive tunneled city were all in tip-top shape, so he couldn't say he was cold—just rather chilled by an unexplained emptiness.

He double-timed his steps, eager to enjoy the warmth of his home and the waiting bottle of liquor. He bumped into a few more people along the way and didn't give a single word of apology. Why should he?

"Doc? Dr. Clock?"

Kennerick turned, rolling his eyes. "What?"

The mail carrier was the sort of man one never quite wanted to touch. He always had a freshly pressed suit and clean nails, nevertheless something about him still made Kennerick uneasy—if Kennerick had been prone to such weak feelings.

"Mail, sir. All pink and nice smelling. From another one of your women?"

Kennerick snatched the flower-decorated envelope, careful not to touch the man's fingers. "What do you know of my women?"

The fool leaned in with a familiarity that rankled Kennerick.

"Well, I sees 'em sneaking out in their frillies every so—"

"The question was rhetorical."

"How you ain't had all them husbands coming here to kill you, I'll never—"

"Go away."

The man mumbling about Kennerick being a "mean bastard," or some such, brought Kennerick's face the first smile all day. Reading the note erased it.

One of the few things that still pleased him was the female form. Women deserved to be enjoyed. Yet, he'd always chosen his dalliances with great care.

The women didn't have to be rich.

They didn't have to be outrageously intelligent.

They did, however, need to be married.

It kept things clean and all the women in their own place.

Dodging angry husbands took too much energy and discretion. Sending indiscreet little notes like the one in his hand wouldn't help the cause. Whoever sent it—well, he would remove them from his mental dance card permanently.

The costly seaweed paper crinkled between his fingers, and he sniffed it, trying to dredge up a memory of the woman behind the inkwell.

Dredge was precisely the word, because he had to dig deep, going back several years.

Smoky. That's what the scent was, but deep and with nose-teasing spices that threw him back to one, raven-haired beauty from his younger days.

He sniffed again. *Oh, yes.* He detected vanilla and ambergris and all manner of unknown zest from Persian Waters.

Hala, the dark heiress who'd carved out his heart, had deigned to contact him. *Damn her!*

He balled the note and tossed it, leaving it for the tunnel sweepers to collect along with the rest of the city's filth during the night. If that bitch thought she could stroll into his life again...well...he'd just have to...well...

Hell.

He hadn't made it a good five steps before turning around to retrieve the note. Not because he cared. If she was desperate enough to contact him, he might as well find out why. He could use a laugh.

Not that she'd made it easy. Typical Hala.

The note itself was a puzzle. It was folded in a square and in such a way one needed a key to open it to avoid ruining the note. Random letters and numbers lined each possible entry point, but every time he lifted an edge, a bit of the paper ripped.

Kennerick rushed into the house and straight to the small laboratory attached to his bedroom. Under a microscope and with lights so bright they burned his eyes, he could just make out the teasing images of invisible ink.

He clanged vials together as he sought a solution —something of the perfect acidity to bring the ink to life.

He found it.

Of course.

His success was part and parcel of being a genius.

But there was more work still, for all this exercise had produced another puzzle piece. A compass rose sizzled to life, quite literally smoking the paper as the chemicals reacted.

He turned the note so that it pointed north, and he looked for the first number in that direction.

Another rip. *Damn.* Two or three more such mistakes and the letter would be lost entirely.

Perhaps then, north wasn't the starting point. It certainly wasn't home for either Kennerick or Hala. They'd both come from the east, his parents from Italy and Hala's directly from Persia.

He rotated the paper and tried again, looking for the first number and lifting the sheet. Beneath it lay a thin sliver of paper. With a set of pincers pulled from his tools, he eased it out, revealing a new truth. The message wasn't the note.

The message was this slip and it was so small that if anyone had simply opened the letter, it would have fallen with the destroyed remainder of the paper. The slip was blank, but he dipped his finger into the same liquid compound then smeared it across the thin paper.

His heart, already frozen, nearly cracked at what he read.

I need you...

The story continues in The Doctor of London, *now available at all retailers and* www.lynbrittan.com/wol

Also available, Steam Me Up, Rawley, by Angela Quarles

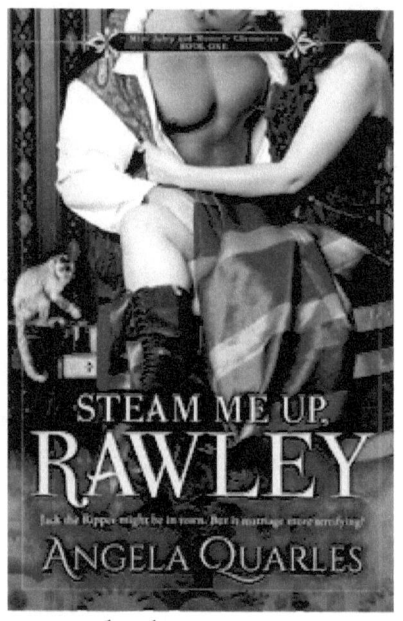

Jack the Ripper might be in town. But is marriage more terrifying?

In an alternate Deep South in 1890, society reporter Adele de la Pointe wants to make her own way in the world, despite her family's pressure to become a society wife. Hoping to ruin herself as a matrimonial prospect, she seizes the opportunity to cover the recent Jack the Ripper-style murders for the newspaper, but her father's dashing new intern suggests a more terrifying headline—marriage!marriage.

Available in ebook and paperback at all major retailers and www.angelaquarles.com

Thank you for reading. Visit
http://lynbrittan.com/newsletter for new release alerts.

Or just stop by and talk about whatever ;)
Twitter: www.twitter.com/LynBrittan
Facebook: www.facebook.com/AuthorLynBrittan
Pinterest: www.pinterest.com/LynBrittan
NSFW Tumblr: www.lynbrittan.Tumblr.com

Did you love *The Clocks of London*? Then you should read *The Doctor of London* by Lyn Brittan!

Kennerick Clock, London's most ornery private investigator, has just received a note from the woman who broke his heart. Lady Hala Javan needs his help and he's willing to give it - for the right price. But if Hala thinks a curiously folded piece of paper can reel back him in, the spoiled brat better think again.

Lady Hala feels about as small as a sea flea for writing Kennerick. Untitled and of common employ, she abandoned him years ago under pressure from her family. Leaving him remains her deepest regret. Now facing an attack on her life, she needs Kennerick.

He's the one man strong and clever enough to save the day. Assuming, of course, he doesn't kill her first.

A Waters of London Novella

Read more at www.lynbrittan.com.

Also by Pamela Lyn

Cape Elizabeth Series
The Prince
The Traitor
The Chosen
The Wolves of Cape Elizabeth: The
Complete Series
Alecto

Lightning Saga
Rafe's Reward
Qiang's Quest
Juan's Journey
Scott's Solace
Lightning Saga Bundle

Waters of London
The Clocks of London

Watch for more at www.pamelalyn.com.

Also by Lyn Brittan

Cape Elizabeth Series
The Prince
The Traitor
The Chosen
Alecto

Lightning Saga
Rafe's Reward
Qiang's Quest
Juan's Journey
Scott's Solace

Outer Settlement Agency
Solia's Moon
Anja's Star
Quinn's Quasar
Lana's Comet
Outer Settlement Agency Omnibus
Vin's Rules
Anja's Star

The Djinn Series
The Genie's Witch
A Genie's Love
The Cowboy Genie's Wife

Waters of London
The Clocks of London
The Doctor of London

Standalone
Moonlit Embrace

Watch for more at www.lynbrittan.com.

About the Author

Lyn grew up in New Orleans and decided to live like her heroes, James Bond and Indiana Jones. She wasn't totally successful and never had to shoot her way out of a hotel bedroom. She's still coming to terms with it.

Read more at www.lynbrittan.com.

9 780692 265420